Sharon Creech

WHO WROTE THAT?

LOUISA MAY ALCOTT,
SECOND EDITION

JANE AUSTEN

AVI

L. FRANK BAUM

JUDY BLUME,
SECOND EDITION

RAY BRADBURY

BETSY BYARS

MEG CABOT

BEVERLY CLEARY

ROBERT CORMIER

BRUCE COVILLE

SHARON CREECH

ROALD DAHL

CHARLES DICKENS

DR. SEUSS,
SECOND EDITION

ERNEST J. GAINES

S.E. HINTON

WILL HOBBS

ANTHONY HOROWITZ

STEPHEN KING

URSULA K. LE GUIN

MADELEINE L'ENGLE

GAIL CARSON LEVINE

C.S. LEWIS,
SECOND EDITION

LOIS LOWRY

ANN M. MARTIN

STEPHENIE MEYER

L.M. MONTGOMERY

PAT MORA

WALTER DEAN MYERS

ANDRE NORTON

SCOTT O'DELL

CHRISTOPHER PAOLINI

BARBARA PARK

KATHERINE PATERSON

GARY PAULSEN

RICHARD PECK

TAMORA PIERCE

DAVID "DAV" PILKEY

EDGAR ALLAN POE

BEATRIX POTTER

PHILIP PULLMAN

MYTHMAKER:
THE STORY OF
J.K. ROWLING,
SECOND EDITION

MAURICE SENDAK

SHEL SILVERSTEIN

LEMONY SNICKET

GARY SOTO

JERRY SPINELLI

R.L. STINE

EDWARD L.
STRATEMEYER

MARK TWAIN

H.G. WELLS

E.B. WHITE

LAURA INGALLS
WILDER

JACQUELINE WILSON

LAURENCE YEP

JANE YOLEN

Sharon Creech

Tracey Baptiste

Foreword by
Kyle Zimmer

CHELSEA HOUSE
An Infobase Learning Company

Sharon Creech

Chelsea House
An imprint of Infobase Learning
132 West 31st Street
New York, NY 10001

Library of Congress Cataloging-in-Publication Data
Baptiste, Tracey.
 Sharon Creech / by Tracey Baptiste.
 p. cm. — (Who wrote that?)
 Includes bibliographical references and index.
 ISBN 978-1-60413-774-3
 1. Creech, Sharon—Juvenile literature. 2. Authors, American—20th century—Biography—Juvenile literature. 3. Young adult fiction—Authorship—Juvenile literature. I. Title. II. Series.
 PS3553.R3373Z57 2011
 813'.54—dc22
 [B]   2010030595

Chelsea House books are available at special discounts when purchased in bulk quantities for business, associations, institutions, or sales promotions. Please call our Special Sales Department in New York at (212) 967-8800 or (800) 322-8755.

You can find Chelsea House on the World Wide Web at
http://www.infobaselearning.com.

Text design by Keith Trego
Cover design by Alicia Post
Composition by EJB Publishing Services
Cover printed by Yurchak Printing, Landisville, Pa.
Book printed and bound by Yurchak Printing, Landisville, Pa.
Date printed: May 2011
Printed in the United States of America

10 9 8 7 6 5 4 3 2 1

This book is printed on acid-free paper.

All links and Web addresses were checked and verified to be correct at the time of publication. Because of the dynamic nature of the Web, some addresses and links may have changed since publication and may no longer be valid.

Table of Contents

FOREWORD BY
KYLE ZIMMER
PRESIDENT, FIRST BOOK

HUMANITY IS POWERED by stories. From our earliest days as thinking beings, we employed every available tool to tell each other stories. We danced, drew pictures on the walls of our caves, spoke, and sang. All of this extraordinary effort was designed to entertain, recount the news of the day, explain natural occurrences—and then gradually to build religious and cultural traditions and establish the common bonds and continuity that eventually formed civilizations. Stories are the most powerful force in the universe; they are the primary element that has distinguished our evolutionary path.

Our love of the story has not diminished with time. Enormous segments of societies are devoted to the art of storytelling. Book sales in the United States alone topped $24 billion in 2006; movie studios spend fortunes to create and promote stories; and the news industry is more pervasive in its presence than ever before.

There is no mystery to our fascination. Great stories are magic. They can introduce us to new cultures, or remind us of the nobility and failures of our own, inspire us to greatness or scare us to death; but above all, stories provide human insight on a level that is unavailable through any other source. In fact, stories connect each of us to the rest of humanity not just in our own time, but also throughout history.

This special magic of books is the greatest treasure that we can hand down from generation to generation. In fact, that spark in a child that comes from books became the motivation for the creation of my organization, First Book, a national literacy program with a simple mission: to provide new books to the most disadvantaged children. At present, First Book has been at work in hundreds of communities for over a decade. Every year children in need receive millions of books through our organization and millions more are provided through dedicated literacy institutions across the United States and around the world. In addition, groups of people dedicate themselves tirelessly to working with children to share reading and stories in every imaginable setting from schools to the streets. Of course, this Herculean effort serves many important goals. Literacy translates to productivity and employability in life and many other valid and even essential elements. But at the heart of this movement are people who love stories, love to read, and want desperately to ensure that no one misses the wonderful possibilities that reading provides.

When thinking about the importance of books, there is an overwhelming urge to cite the literary devotion of great minds. Some have written of the magnitude of the importance of literature. Amy Lowell, an American poet, captured the concept when she said, "Books are more than books. They are the life, the very heart and core of ages past, the reason why men lived and worked and died, the essence and quintessence of their lives." Others have spoken of their personal obsession with books, as in Thomas Jefferson's simple statement: "I live for books." But more compelling, perhaps, is the almost instinctive excitement in children for books and stories.

Throughout my years at First Book, I have heard truly extraordinary stories about the power of books in the lives of children. In one case, a homeless child, who had been bounced from one location to another, later resurfaced—and the only possession that he had fought to keep was the book he was given as part of a First Book distribution months earlier. More recently, I met a child who, upon receiving the book he wanted, flashed a big smile and said, "This is my big chance!" These snapshots reveal the true power of books and stories to give hope and change lives.

As these children grow up and continue to develop their love of reading, they will owe a profound debt to those volunteers who reached out to them—a debt that they may repay by reaching out to spark the next generation of readers. But there is a greater debt owed by all of us—a debt to the storytellers, the authors, who have bound us together, inspired our leaders, fueled our civilizations, and helped us put our children to sleep with their heads full of images and ideas.

WHO WROTE THAT? is a series of books dedicated to introducing us to a few of these incredible individuals. While we have almost always honored stories, we have not uniformly honored storytellers. In fact, some of the most important authors have toiled in complete obscurity throughout their lives or have been openly persecuted for the uncomfortable truths that they have laid before us. When confronted with the magnitude of their written work or perhaps the daily grind of our own, we can forget that writers are people. They struggle through the same daily indignities and dental appointments, and they experience the intense joy and bottomless despair that many of us do. Yet somehow they rise above it all to deliver a powerful thread that connects us all. It is a rare honor to have the opportunity that these books provide to share the lives of these extraordinary people. Enjoy.

The American children's book author Sharon Creech has won numerous awards for her work, including the Newbery Medal and Carnegie Medal. In 1995, Walk Two Moons *earned her the Newbery; in 2002, she received the Carnegie for* Ruby Holler.

1

Wandering Through Books

"YOU KNOW, I WROTE a lot because my father for the last six years of his life couldn't speak. And I felt like, it was really as soon as he died that I started writing, that I was using the words he couldn't use,"[1] recalled Sharon Creech in a 2009 interview with the children's book Web site Twenty by Jenny. During the interview, she was sitting on a hotel bed with her American editor, Joanna Cotler of HarperCollins Publishers. After more than 15 years of working together, the two women had the easy back-and-forth manner of longtime friends, and it was clear they respected and trusted each other.

They recalled conversations during which Cotler expressed concern about what Creech was writing next, as well as their first phone call, back when *Walk Two Moons* was being edited. When Cotler approached the then-unknown Creech, the author hoped that Cotler would not change any of her words. Since then, Creech has learned to trust Cotler's judgment, and Cotler has learned to trust Creech's process, knowing that what will come out of their collaborations will be some of the most well-loved stories of this generation.

EVERYDAY JOURNEYS

Though Creech credits her father for jump-starting her writing, her interest in becoming an author began long before his death in 1992. It began, as much of Creech's work does, with the journey. "I think the journey image is instinctive," said Creech in her Newbery acceptance speech for *Walk Two Moons.*

> Journeys have always been important to me. When I was young, the trips my family took every summer allowed me to see a wider world. When my children and I journeyed to England and Switzerland, we learned so much and were changed so much by what we saw. And when I studied literature, I saw how frequently that image of the journey is used to convey interior journeys as well.[2]

As Creech writes these stories of traveling characters, she asks her readers to come along as well. As Creech, her protagonist, and the reader travel together, they are all learning something about themselves. These journeys very closely match the kinds of journeys that Creech became used to in her life, both as a young girl in the backseat of her parents' car and as an adult, traveling the world with her children. Creech later used what she and her family were learning then to feed the interior and exterior journeys of her heroes and heroines. And in so doing, she was able to tap into experiences that were real in her own life, translate them to the page, and then touch something real in her readers as well.

"I . . . love the way that each book—any book—is its own journey," she said in a 2001 interview with *Publishers Weekly*. "You open it, and off you go. You are changed in some way, large or small, by having traveled with those characters."[3] As a writer, she is brought on a journey by her characters that is just as exciting for her,

Did you know...

Many writers work with several editors and different publishing houses throughout their careers. Sharon Creech, however, has mostly worked with one American editor, Joanna Cotler, and one publisher, Harper-Collins, for as long as she has been writing children's books. Her relationship with Cotler had an odd beginning. George Nicholson and David Gale bought the manuscript, but they both left HarperCollins shortly after acquiring it. Creech therefore was given a new editor, Nancy Siscoe, but she left as well. Marilyn Kriney, who was president of HarperCollins at the time, introduced Creech to Cotler. The two have continued to collaborate almost exclusively ever since.

as she is discovering it through writing, as it is for the reader after the book is finished. "It was inevitable that the characters and I would also have interior journeys on these treks, and for me that is much of the excitement of writing: discovering what the interior journey is, how it changes the traveler,"[4] Creech added in her Newbery speech. Creech's method of bringing these extraordinary journeys to books has brought her great literary success. Her first novel for young adults published in the United States earned her a Newbery award; since then, Creech's novels have continued to earn not only literary accolades but also the love of her young readers.

Since Creech and Joanna Cotler began their collaboration, Creech has written 17 books for young adults. Most of them have been award winners or have gotten rave reviews from both professionals and her army of devoted fans. Not all of them, however, are straight prose. *Love That Dog* and its companion book, *Hate That Cat*, are both written in verse.

Creech has also written plays. In the collection *Acting Out*, Creech and some of her contemporary young adult

Did you know...

Sharon Creech loves to read books for young adults as much as she enjoys writing them. Among her favorite books for young people are Karen Hesse's *Out of the Dust* and *Witness*, Jerry Spinelli's *Loser* and *Maniac Magee*, and Christopher Paul Curtis's *The Watsons Go to Birmingham—1963*.

authors wrote plays for young actors that all had a series of words, chosen by the authors, as a common thread. Her 2005 book, *Replay*, is not only about a play but also includes the actual play at the end for readers to act out. Though her novel *Walk Two Moons* was not written as a play, it was later adapted into one and put on as an off-Broadway theater production.

ALL THE DIFFERENT LEVELS

Since her writing career took off in the mid-1990s, Creech has written at nearly breakneck speed, producing at least one book per year. It is a wonder that Creech is able to write so much and so well; her secret weapon is the wealth of experiences that she has culled in her travels. Creech has an extraordinary ability to use the threads of her experiences and weave them seamlessly into her books, creating a deep and rich tapestry that serves as a backdrop for her characters.

Her first published young adult novel, *Absolutely Normal Chaos*, describes a family growing up in Ohio, where Creech was born and raised. The three brothers in the book even take on the names of Creech's three younger siblings. *Walk Two Moons* and *Ruby Holler* also take place in the American Midwest and use descriptions of places Creech loved growing up. In *Bloomability* and *The Wanderer*, Creech turned to more exotic settings, but still used familiar venues. The grandfather's house in *The Wanderer* is a perfect description of Creech's own house in England, and the boarding school in *Bloomability* is similar to the one she taught at while living in Switzerland. Even the title *Bloomability* was inspired by a student she had, who could not pronounce the word *possibility* and said *bloomability* instead. *The Wanderer* describes a cross-Atlantic sea voyage. While Creech herself did not sail across the Atlantic, her daughter did, and Creech used that experience, including the nearly disastrous storm that occurred, to craft the plot of the novel.

In an interview conducted before Creech embarked on her book tour for *The Unfinished Angel*, Joanna Cotler said:

> This is what I find so fascinating now with her [writing] process. Because by the time something comes to me, Sharon has managed to pull together all these things [in her life] into a story. And from all these different unconscious ideas and subjects and non-thoughts comes this story . . . that really by the time it gets to me, I can see all the different levels that [she has] been thinking.[5]

To get a better understanding of the wealth of experiences that Creech has brought to her books, we would have to go back to the beginning and look at Creech's life as a young girl. It is clear that her writing life began as a child—she may have honed her writing skills in competition with her four siblings as they each tried to tell stories and be heard. And later in her life, as Creech traveled all over the world, she brought her wandering experiences to her writing, which allowed her readers to wander through her books.

During her childhood, Sharon Creech traveled often to visit her extended family, some of whom lived on a farm like the one pictured here. These youthful experiences would eventually find their way into her writing.

2

The Journey Begins

"I WANTED TO BE many things when I grew up: a painter, an ice skater, a singer, a teacher, and a reporter. It soon became apparent that I had little drawing talent, very limited tolerance for falling on ice, and absolutely no ability to stay on key while singing,"[1] says Sharon Creech on her official Web site. But as a child, Creech did not seem to dwell too much on the things she might do as a grown-up. She was too busy having fun with her four siblings. On her Web site, she describes her early life in a Cleveland suburb as growing up "with my noisy and rowdy family."[2]

Creech was born in South Euclid, Ohio, on July 29, 1945. Her parents were Ann and Arvel Creech; Sharon was their second child. She went to Shore Elementary across the street from her house, and then to Oxford Elementary School in Cleveland Heights. After second grade, she and her family moved to a larger house on Buxton Road in South Euclid, in order to accommodate her new younger brothers. It was in South Euclid that she spent the bulk of her childhood years. In the house on Buxton Road, she finished elementary school at Victory Park Elementary School.

Creech says that her book *Absolutely Normal Chaos* is a fictionalized account of her life in South Euclid with her rambunctious family—the setting is based on her own house on Buxton Road, and as a matter of fact, the words *absolutely normal chaos* turn up several times in interviews when Creech is describing her young life. The chaos must have been very inspirational, because this is the time period that Creech reaches back to every time she writes a book for children: "I'm particularly interested in those pivotal ages from nine to fourteen," Creech said, "where a child is no longer a child and not yet an adult, and is just beginning to question, 'Who am I?' 'What will I be?' 'What will I do?' That's pretty much the search for all my narrators."[3] Her mostly female, mainly 13-year-old protagonists seem to have been carved out of the experiences she had during those years of her life. And her characters' warm and loving families appear as a written monument to the large family she enjoyed as a child.

"We had a large, affectionate, extended family that gathered often,"[4] Creech said. The Creech family drove to visit aunts, uncles, cousins, and grandparents in the summers, and the kids spent a lot of time with their cousins, some of whom lived on a farm. They would play outside in the hills, climb trees, swim at a nearby swimming hole, and play in the barn. All day they would run outside, and at night, the family would gather together on the porch to tell stories. During these sessions, young Sharon perfected her storytelling out of necessity. With four siblings and several more cousins, if she could not tell a really engaging story, her voice would never be heard. Those nights on the farm porch were probably the beginning of her life as a writer: "I learned to exaggerate and embellish, because if you didn't, your story was drowned out by someone else's more exciting one."[5] For Sharon, these trips that her family took to visit their grandparents, aunts, uncles, and cousins were pivotal.

"I spent many wild days as a child, running through the hills,"[6] Creech says of her childhood. She seems to yearn for that time when kids were able to go outside and play all day the way she did when she was young. As an adult, she continually writes about heroes and heroines who still enjoy that kind of freedom. The far more restricted life of a modern child in America was a surprise to Creech, after living in Europe for many years and being able to roam freely. On her return to the United States, Creech told *Time* that "there were all these frazzled parents who spent their lives in car pools, getting their kids to ballet lessons and gymnastics. And I was thinking, Goodness, don't the kids ever get time just to climb a tree or lie in the grass? There doesn't seem to be that kind of time for kids anymore."[7] Creech reprises this sentiment in one of her picture books, *A Fine, Fine School.* In it, the heroine protests to the school headmaster, "I haven't learned how to climb very high in my tree," she says. "And I haven't learned how to sit in my tree for a whole hour."[8] The head-master, like the parents Creech observed on her return to the United States, seems oblivious to the simple pleasures that can really make a child's life pleasant. In the novel, an illustration on the lunchroom wall asks, "Why not study while you chew?"

THE FIRST SPARK

"In the summer, we usually took a trip, all of us piled in a car and heading out to Wisconsin or Michigan or, once, to Idaho,"[9] she wrote in her online biography. She remembered the trips being so noisy that she had wondered how her own parents managed to put up with it—especially in the close confines of the car. Creech describes one summer in particular when the family took that onetime trip to Idaho. She turned 12 during the trip. It was five days in the car, going across six states. The trip that summer, Creech said, "had a powerful effect"[10] on her. She was amazed at how big the country was as they drove through it.

> ## Did you know...
>
> The farm where Sharon Creech's cousins lived, and where some of her family still lives, is in Quincy, Kentucky. That farm has made it into four of her books in fictional form as Bybanks, Kentucky. It has appeared in *Walk Two Moons*, *Chasing Redbird*, *Bloom-ability*, and *The Wanderer*. In *The Wanderer*, the farm is not mentioned by name, but only referenced.

As they traveled from Ohio to Lewiston, Idaho, where her extended family lived, Creech's family stopped at a Native American reservation. It was July 29, 1957, the author's twelfth birthday. She had always wanted a pair of moccasins of her own, and she had finally found a pair of soft leather ones. "I loved moccasins because I thought one of my ancestors was an American Indian," Creech told *The Reading Teacher* in 1996. "I exaggerated this possibility, and I would tell people that I was full-blooded Indian. I would read Indian myths. I was convinced that I was an Indian."[11]

Her early interest in Native American culture helped influence her later views and writing. "My cousins maintain that one of our ancestors was an American Indian," she said in her Newbery speech. "I inhaled Indian myths, and among my favorites were those which involved stories of reincarnation." Because she believed that American Indians climbed trees, she says, "I think I spent half my childhood up a tree."[12]

Her love of Native American lore and this particular five-day trip had a tremendous impact on Creech, who later turned her memories of the journey into her second children's book. The events of that summer came back to her 30 years later as she was struggling to write her second children's book, *Walk Two Moons*. With that book, she won her first, and possibly her best, accolades when it was awarded the Newbery Medal. But Creech the writer was still a long way off the summer she traveled to Idaho. She may have been vying for attention during storytelling competitions with her family members, but she had not yet fostered a love of literature.

"At home, we five siblings were usually urged to 'go outside and play!' This was fine with me. The only books I remember being in our house were a set of the Great Books.

As a child and a teenager, Sharon Creech loved drifting into the kind of magical worlds described in many books, including Ivanhoe, *a novel written by Sir Walter Scott in 1820. The cover illustration of this 1960 edition is by Henri Dimpre.*

These included the works of Sophocles, Plato, etc.—not exactly light reading. I remember pulling one of the volumes out one day, determined to read Plato, and as I did so, a centipede scurried across the cover and onto my leg. I didn't go anywhere near those Great Books for a long, long time,"[13] said Creech in an online interview for her publisher HarperTeen. After the centipede fiasco, Sharon found books at school to read.

Fortunately her next encounter with literature had a delightful impact, one that may have allowed her to recreate for her own readers the feeling of losing oneself in a story. In the same interview for HarperTeen, Creech recalls reading *The Timbertoes* by Edna M. Aldredge and Jessie F. McKee, a book that she says was likely her first chapter book. She especially enjoyed the colorful illustrations done by John Gee. She noted, "I think this was my first sense of being immersed in a story that I could read by myself."[14] It was the first of many books in which she lost herself. "I don't remember the titles of books I read as a child," Creech said, "but I do remember the experience of reading—of drifting into the pages and living in someone else's world, the excitement of never knowing what lay ahead."[15] She did in fact remember a few titles: Besides *The Timbertoes*, there was *Ivanhoe*, a novel written by Sir Walter Scott in 1820, which she read as a teen. She recalled, "These were all magical worlds, full of mystery and imagination: anything could happen, anything at all."[16]

HOOKED ON FICTION

The Timbertoes and *Ivanhoe* sparked young Sharon's love of stories, and fortunately for her vast number of fans, it did not end there. Creech credits her sixth-grade teacher Ms. Zolar for giving her encouragement, and even mentions her

favorite teacher in her first book for children, *Absolutely Normal Chaos.*

At age 12, Sharon developed an interest in reporting and decided to report on the goings-on of her neighborhood. "I soon found that I would make a terrible reporter," she told the *Mason Gazette*, her graduate school alumni newspaper. "I didn't like the facts, so I changed them."[17] As a girl, she made up incredible stories about the people in her South Euclid neighborhood. Often, she would pen funny poems and give them away as gifts. In the summers, she and her siblings would write plays and act them out for any family and friends who were interested. In high school, another of her teachers piqued her interest in poetry. She began

Did you know...

The Timbertoes was originally published in 1932 by The Harter Publishing Company, but it became popular when it appeared as a serial comic strip in *Highlights*, a magazine for children. For more than 30 years, the cartoon family, Ma and Pa, their children Mabel and Tommy, and their pets Spot the dog and Splinter the cat—who look like they have been carved out of wood—have been a part of *Highlights*. They first appeared only in black-and-white line drawings, but in 2003, *Highlights* switched the strip to digital color. After the original illustrator, John Gee, died, *Highlights* tapped Judith Hunt, and more recently Ron Zalme, to take over the drawings.

to enjoy the rhythms, sounds, and emotions employed in poetic writing, and years later, when Creech was an adult, she was still so intrigued by what she had learned in high school that she decided to write poetry.

As a teen, Creech was very solitary. She recalled, "I always thought that everyone else knew something that I didn't; that there must be a manual out there that I didn't have access to! I still feel that way some days."[18] Creech echoes this sentiment in *Absolutely Normal Chaos*, when Mary Lou Finney says, "I wish there was a manual for this sort of thing,"[19] as she navigates her first romance with a boy from school. Today, Creech readily recognizes that her time as a youth is fodder for her writing: "I'm . . . sort of plumbing my own past—how I became who I am, and how I became aware of the world."[20]

Sharon went through her high school years as a hall monitor and an office aide, and although they might have seemed like dull jobs, she really enjoyed the work. At home she helped to care for her three younger brothers, especially when her older sister, Sandy, went off to college. After Sharon graduated from Brush High School in 1963, she followed her sister to nearby Hiram College in Ohio. Once there, she had no idea what she wanted to do. She recalled, "I told a roommate that I wanted to try every job there was for three months at a time. I was interested in all sorts of jobs: writing, painting, house-building, tree-trimming, teaching, acting."[21] It was a list similar to the one she kept as a young child. But she need not have worried. Her calling eventually found her.

She recalled, "It was in college, when I took literature and writing courses, that I became intrigued by story-telling."[22] In her last year at college, she finally got around to taking a writing class. On the first day, her professor, a visiting British writer, gave the class their assignment for the semester. It was simple: They were to write a novel. The first chapter was due in one week. Creech had no idea what to do and spent the week re-creating the dramatic scenes of writers she had seen in movies. She would sit at her typewriter, type up a page of writing, then rip it out of the machine, crumple it up, and dash it dramatically to the ground. But at the end of the week, all the drama had wrought nothing. She did not have a first chapter to bring to class.

Finally she decided to be herself and write about something that had happened the summer before. Her first line was, "Last summer we drove from Ohio to Mexico."[23] It was a story about the summer she and her boyfriend spent in an old, nearly worn-out Volkswagen. She changed the names, beefed up the details, and handed it in. She found praise for her work and valuable criticism she remembers even today: "The first long story I wrote in college received much praise, but also this note: Your characters' names are so boring. I have tried not to make that mistake again."[24] She heeded her professor's advice. Truly, with character names like Salamanca Tree Hiddle and Miss Stretchberry, it is nearly impossible to imagine anyone considering her characters' names to be boring.

Her professor also noted that her story followed the archetypal journey structure—a story that is based on where the characters go and what happens to them along the way. Creech notes:

> The journey as a motif—as a literary convention—really appeals to me. The physical journey is always a metaphor for the interior journey. And perhaps because I lived so much of

my life outside of my home country, I am in tune to this notion that, as you go, you are learning something not only about the world, but also about yourself in the process.[25]

Orson Welles was an acclaimed actor and director, best known for his work on such films as Citizen Kane, The Magnificent Ambersons, *and* Touch of Evil. *While working at the Federal Theater Project archives in graduate school, Sharon Creech catalogued some of Welles's original illustrations for costume and set designs.*

3

Traveling to
Far-off Lands

SHARON CREECH GRADUATED from Hiram College in 1967 with a bachelor's degree in English literature. Shortly thereafter, she and her boyfriend, H.R. Leuthy Jr., got married and moved to Washington, D.C., where Leuthy had gotten a job. Their two children were born shortly after marriage: Robert in 1968 and Karin in 1971. Though Creech wanted to pursue a graduate degree, she decided to wait until both children were old enough for school. She then enrolled at George Mason University in Fairfax, Virginia, just outside their home in Washington, D.C. There, Creech could take classes at night. Once again, she majored in English literature. She wanted to be immersed in stories: "To be able to create other worlds, to be able to explore mystery and myth—I couldn't imagine a better way to live . . . except perhaps to be a teacher, because teachers got to handle books all day long."[1]

Creech had fallen in love with literature and writing. At George Mason that love was nourished with a lot of encouragement for her writing from her professors. It was also at George Mason that she came to understand how writers need to read a lot in order to write well: "I studied writing with Don Gallehr, and I studied writing-by-way-of-literature (literature courses from which I learned a lot about writing) with Peter Brunette, John O'Connor, and Lorraine Brown—all truly excellent teachers, each of whom took my thinking to a deeper level."[2]

Another of her teachers, a visiting writer named John Gardener, taught Creech more about the archetypal structures of stories, specifically how the journey structure was one in which the protagonist goes on both a literal and an internal quest. She would rely on this structure for all of her novels. In the second archetypal structure, the so-called stranger-comes-to-town type, a new person enters the protagonist's life and changes him somehow.

At the same time, Creech also began to write poetry and had some of her poems published in college journals. They were Creech's first publications as a writer. She also had another first experience in graduate school: Remembering the plays she had written with her siblings in South Euclid, she longed to write a real play, and worked with a theater project to gain experience. So, in the last two years of her graduate school career, she worked at the Federal Theater Project archives. There she learned as much as she could about the theater, and she got a chance to see plays in action. On the Barnes and Noble Web site, Creech revealed that this was one of her most interesting jobs: "I catalogued original illustrations for set and costume designs, some by [famed filmmaker] Orson Welles. It was fascinating work!"[3] She would later put what she learned at the theater archives to work in her writing life.

TURNING POINTS

Creech graduated from George Mason University with a master's degree in English literature in 1978. Like her last year of college, 1978 turned out to be another pivotal one for Creech. After a difficult 10-year marriage, she divorced her husband and began to care for their two children on her own. She also needed to find a new job to take care of herself and her family. She realized too late that teaching would have been the perfect job for her, but since she had no educational experience and had graduated without a teaching degree, she believed it was probably out of the question. Then a friend of hers, who was working at the American School in Switzerland (TASIS) in one of their schools near London, wrote her a letter. The letter told Creech about a teaching job that luckily did not require a teaching degree, and it let her know that the headmaster would be in the United States soon to recruit new teachers. Her friend said, "Our school needs you to teach children to write. And to teach English."[4] The position of English literature teacher only required that the teacher be trained in that area. It was perfect for Creech. She liked the idea of being a literature teacher and warmed quickly to the thought of living in another country. She set up the interview and met with the headmaster, but by the end, things had not gone quite as she had planned.

"I was steamed,"[5] Creech said of her feelings after the interview. The headmaster was concerned that a single mother of two young children would not be able to handle the rigors of a teaching job. He underestimated Creech's determination, as well as her writing skills. Creech wanted him to get the point that she was perfect for the TASIS position, and she put her feelings into words, writing a letter to the headmaster the night after their meeting, in which she described exactly why she was perfect for the job. Creech was willing to make the move to England, not so much because she felt brave, but because she realized it would provide a better life for her young children. "I could give the kids something that I couldn't have given them if I'd stayed in the States,"[6] she recalled in a 2001 interview. Her letter worked. The headmaster offered Creech the job, and she was suddenly staring an entirely new life in the face, all because of that one convincing

Did you know...

The American School in Switzerland (TASIS) was founded in 1956 by M. Christ Fleming, who wanted to create an American school abroad to allow American students to experience European culture. Since that time, it has developed further to foster camaraderie in all cultures. TASIS is the oldest American boarding school in Europe. Classes begin at the Pre-K level and continue through high school. Students can board there throughout the school year, starting in seventh grade. TASIS now has schools in Switzerland, England, and Puerto Rico, and teaches students from approximately 50 different nations.

piece of writing. Creech had no idea that in a few years, she would be known for making people believe in whatever she put down on paper.

"The most important piece of writing that Sharon has ever produced is the letter that she wrote to the headmaster back in 1979, convincing him to offer her a job in England."[7] That opinion came from Lyle Rigg, who ultimately had the most to gain from Creech's move to the United Kingdom that year, although at the time, neither he nor Creech had any idea her move would affect both of their lives. He wrote, "If Sharon were not such a skilled writer, we probably would never have met. . . . Although I have never read Sharon's letter to that headmaster, I have heard that it was a masterpiece of persuasion and was instrumental in her being hired."[8] It was fortune, too, that brought Lyle Rigg to TASIS the same year as Creech. The headmaster who had given Creech a hard time before offering her the job also hired Rigg to work at the school as the assistant headmaster. Rigg met Creech in 1979 when they both started working at the school, and three years later, in 1982, the two were married. But that was still to come.

CREECH TEACHES

Creech and her two children, Rob and Karin, arrived in England with £20 in her pocket—the equivalent of about $28—and a salary of £5,000 (about $7,000) a year, which was then enough to rent an apartment and take care of herself and her family. They moved into a small village in Surrey, England, which had one shop, a 300-year-old house, a 1,000-year-old church, and the school itself, which was situated in a Georgian mansion with expansive green lawns. The neighbors were, as the author recalled, "nice, hardworking people, raising their children, sweeping their

Seen here, traditional architecture in the old village of Shere in Surrey, England. When Sharon Creech moved to Surrey to teach, she found herself immediately falling in love with her new home.

steps and growing their flowers," and with nearby places of great literature, like Stratford-upon-Avon, where William Shakespeare lived and performed his plays, she thought she had "landed in heaven."[9]

Her love of her new home eventually seeped into the pages of her books, as evidenced by certain passages of *The Wanderer.* "The houses all have names like Glenacre and The Yellow Cottage and The Green Cottage and The Old Post Office,"[10] Sophie, Creech's protagonist, describes when she and her family finally arrive in England near the end of the book. Sophie goes on to describe her grandfather's house. "It's so pretty here, with roses climbing up the side of the house, and lavender spreading in big clumps along the walk, and inside are tiny rooms and wee windows and miniature fireplaces."[11] The house Creech describes is really the house that she and Lyle Rigg lived in when they taught at TASIS. Built in the seventeenth century, it was called Walnut Tree Cottage.

Creech and her family adjusted well to their new life in England. Creech found herself enjoying her life even as she became accustomed to the rigors of teaching. She found time to give her children the kind of freedom of movement that she had enjoyed as a child. Today, she remembers great moments that they shared, like one that occurred two months after their arrival in England: She took the children to Lands' End, a small settlement. After the long car ride, her daughter, Karin, ran out of the car and toward the green sea, shouting, "I'm free! I'm free!" Creech said, "I have carried this beautiful image with me. All children need this—a place where you can feel free, where you don't have to have this: 'Don't spill your tea/ Say thank you'; where you can, for a while, spit. I think they should have that every day."[12]

But she and her family were not to live in wonder at their new home for long. Just as Sophie experienced a black wave crashing down in *The Wanderer*, there was trouble brewing for Creech and her family. She recalled:

> In 1980, when my children and I had been in England for nine months, my father had a stroke. Although he lived for six more years, the stroke left him paralyzed and unable to speak. Think of all the words we wanted to say to him, and all the words he must have wanted to say to us. Think of all those words locked up for six years, because his mind could neither accept nor deliver words.[13]

The inability of her father to process words affected Creech deeply.

Did you know...

Many of the books that Sharon Creech taught in her classroom inspired her in her writing life. The plot of Chaucer's *The Canterbury Tales* inspired the structure of pilgrimage that Zinny takes in *Chasing Redbird*. A discussion with her class about the ghost in Shakespeare's *Hamlet* inspired the ghost in *Pleasing the Ghost*. Homer's poem about an epic sea voyage, *The Odyssey*, shows up in *Absolutely Normal Chaos* as a book that Mary Lou Finney reads for a literature assignment, and the idea of the sea voyage also inspired Creech's Newbery Honor book, *The Wanderer*. *Love That Dog* was a direct response to reading one of Walter Dean Myers's poems, "Love That Boy."

Geoffrey Chaucer was a fourteenth-century English poet, soldier, and diplomat, who is today best known for penning The Canterbury Tales, *a work of literature taught and beloved by many literature teachers, including Sharon Creech.*

Despite her troubles, Creech concentrated on being a teacher, and despite not having been trained to teach children, she turned out to be great at it, mostly because she was determined to be just that. "I love kids and I love literature," she told the *Times* of London.

> When I taught, it was as if I was going to correct everything that teachers had done wrong with my son who had such a hard time at school. In an American state school he had been told at six that he did not learn normally, while his eight-year-old sister was castigated for writing too slowly. I was going to be for kids what those teachers were not.[14]

She knew many teachers that were great, and during her teaching years at TASIS, she met even more. But she was certainly frustrated with her children's experiences in education. Creech tried to provide a broad experience for her students and an understanding of their individual selves, which she felt her own children had not always experienced.

Lyle Rigg recalled:

> As a teacher of American and British literature to American and international teenagers, Sharon has shared her love both of literature and of writing. She'd open up [Geoffrey] Chaucer's world in *The Canterbury Tales* and then head off to Canterbury with her students so that they could make the pilgrimage themselves. She'd offer *Hamlet*, and then off they would all go to Stratford-upon-Avon.[15]

The reason that Creech taught such great but difficult authors like Chaucer and Shakespeare so well was because she knew how they would translate to the lives of her teenage students. "Everyone understands revenge in

Hamlet," she said. "They don't have to understand every word, but if they're interested in the idea they will want to learn."[16] A difficult syllabus would turn into something really interesting for Creech's students because of her approach to the material—but her teaching days were not going to last forever.

Sharon Creech won a Newbery Award for Walk Two Moons, a novel first published in 1994 that was inspired by her love of Native American lore and the cross-country trips she took during her childhood.

4

Becoming a Writer

After Lyle Rigg and Sharon Creech were married in 1982, he was offered a position at the TASIS school in Switzerland. Creech and her children packed up and went along with him to Montagnola, Switzerland, that same year. Creech taught at the Swiss school while Rigg served as headmaster. Their experiences there would wind up in another of Creech's novels, *Bloomability*. After two years in Switzerland, Rigg was transferred back to the school in England, so they moved again. Creech's new family was getting along well, but at the same time, Creech had little or no time to nurture her own love of writing—and her husband noticed.

Rigg recalled, "Not surprisingly (and just as the headmaster had warned), the demands of motherhood and a full-time teaching position left Sharon with little time for herself—let alone for her writing. Even less time was available after Sharon and I were married."[1] But after the children went off to college back in the United States, Creech found herself with more time to write. After her father died unexpectedly in 1986, following the stroke he had suffered six years earlier, Creech began to concentrate fully on her own writing.

"The connection between my father's death and my flood of writing might be that I had been confronted with the dark wall of mortality: we don't have endless time to follow our dreams,"[2] she said. She began with poetry, and Rigg remembers her writing a lot of it. There were titles like "The Sun on the Bottom" and "Strip Tease" and "Victor, Victorious." But it was in 1988 that she got the encouragement she really needed to pursue it in earnest.

The phone call came out of nowhere, and it notified Creech that one of her poems, titled "Cleansing," had been awarded the Billee Murray Denny Poetry Award. The award was sponsored by Lincoln College in Illinois; it was a cash payment of $1,000. Rigg said that winning the award was a turning point for Creech, who had been steadily ramping up her writing efforts. But for her, the effect was not as sudden as Rigg might have thought. She recalled:

> For fifteen years I taught American and British literature, as well as creative writing, to high school juniors and seniors in Europe. I not only learned a lot about great literature but also about people from all over the world and about writing. There came a point when I'd soaked up so much that it all came spilling back out in poems and short stories and novels. The transition from teacher to writer was gradual

(over the course of seven or eight years) and felt like a natural progression.[3]

As she continued to teach and assist her headmaster husband in his work, Creech wrote as much as she could. Prior to winning the poetry award, she had completed a novel titled *The Recital*, which was a serious story about an eccentric woman living in a small town. After it was finished, Creech wanted to try her hand at something more humorous, so she started to work on *Absolutely Normal Chaos*, a reprisal of her youth in South Euclid, Ohio. She admitted that she did it because she was homesick and lonely for her family back in the United States: "Writing the story was a way for me to feel as if my family were with me, right there in our little cottage in England."[4] At the time she was writing this book, she was encouraging her students to keep journals, so Creech decided to put her own teaching to task and write the novel in journal format. She later said that this novel, her first for teens, was "largely influenced by the remembered chaotic tone of my own family."[5] The number of the heroine's house, 4059, is the address of Creech's own childhood home in South Euclid.

Comfortable with what she had written, Creech then sought out a literary agent. Once Creech had secured one, her agent began to submit her work to publishers in the United Kingdom. After about nine months, her agent called to tell her that *The Recital* had been accepted at Pan Macmillan, a British publisher. Not only did the publishing house want her novel, they also gave her a contract to write a second one. Creech went straight to work.

But that was not all. When the editors at Pan Macmillan read *Absolutely Normal Chaos*, they recognized it immediately as a good book for their children's division. "When I wrote *Absolutely Normal Chaos* I didn't know it was a children's book," Creech said. "In that book the girl just happened to be younger."[6] The publisher asked Creech to write another book for young people, but she had no idea that there was even such a thing as a children's division. She knew that if she was going to write another book for children, she had better figure out what a children's book actually was.

The Recital was published in 1990 along with *Absolutely Normal Chaos*. The follow-up to *The Recital*, *Nickel Malley*, about a male protagonist and his relationship with his neighbors, was published a year later. During that time, Creech also fulfilled her desire to write a play with *The Centre of the Universe: Waiting for the Girl*. She was fortunate enough to see it performed in an off-Broadway festival in 1992 in New York City.

WRITING STRUGGLES

Though her path to publication seems like an easy one, Creech did receive her share of rejections. After completing

Did you know...

Pan Macmillan in England published Sharon Creech's first books for adults, *The Recital* and *Nickel Malley*, under her married name, Sharon Rigg. When Creech turned her attention to writing for children, she decided to use her maiden name. Since then, Creech has retained her maiden name throughout her writing career. In fact, her husband, Lyle Rigg, has become accustomed to Creech's fans referring to him as "Mr. Creech!"

and publishing the three novels and one play, she struggled with another book. After writing 800 pages, she showed it to her agent, who was enthusiastic but was unable to get anyone to buy it. After several tries, her agent stopped submitting the manuscript, which ended up as an 800-page clunker at the back of Creech's closet. But although that book had not sold, Creech continued to write.

For her next book, she tried to focus on writing for children as her publisher had asked, but it took her awhile to figure out what writing for children really entailed. She went to a writer's conference and listened to author Lois Lowry speak. (Lowry's novel *The Giver* would later win the Newbery Medal in 1994.) Lowry talked about the elements that go into a book for young people, and Creech knew she had already accomplished that with *Absolutely Normal Chaos*. But now, she needed to put all those elements to work in a second book.

Even though she had already written a book for young adults, Creech found that reassembling the pieces was difficult. She began by trying to write a sequel to *Absolutely Normal Chaos*, but it seemed Mary Lou Finney, the novel's main character, had told as much as she was willing to tell about her own story. Creech managed to write a manuscript, but her agent and her editor at Pan Macmillan did not feel it was strong enough. She revised the manuscript and added a new character, but it still did not work. Then the editor she was working with left, and the new editor still did not like the manuscript. At that point, a frustrated Creech said that she "was ready to toss it into the trash."[7]

GOOD FORTUNE

Creech had already tried and found no success at reviving Mary Lou Finney, the character in her first book, *Absolutely*

Normal Chaos, so she decided to move on. She added a new character, Phoebe Winterbottom, and continued in Phoebe's voice, adding new elements that highlighted Phoebe's own story, including the disappearance of Phoebe's mother. Even though her editor at Pan Macmillan rejected all of these new elements, Creech was determined to continue writing.

Then, out of the blue, she came across a piece of paper from a fortune cookie. She had recently gone to a Chinese restaurant and had slipped the fortune into her bag and forgotten about it. The fortune read, "Don't judge a man until you've walked two moons in his moccasins." Creech wondered what a Native American proverb was doing in a Chinese fortune, but it did not matter. The fortune was precisely what Creech needed. It immediately sparked the memory of herself as a child, wishing to be a Native American. She remembered the summer when she and her family had driven from Ohio to Idaho and the moccasins she had picked up for her twelfth birthday. Her mind began to unconsciously work these elements together while she was still struggling to create a story with Phoebe Winterbottom. Fortunately, Creech discovered a writing method that worked very well for her: She would take naps. She called them "research naps" or "inspiration naps." And after she had taken one, somehow the clouds would have cleared in her thinking and the story would reemerge with some problems solved, and she would be ready to start writing again.

Creech was just beginning to hit her writing stride. Now that her two children were in the United States in college and she had some days that she was not teaching, she used her spare time to concentrate on her writing. So one day, after she had found the fortune and with the stories of Mary

Lou and Phoebe still problems in her head, she took a nap and this line came to her: "Gramps says that I am a country girl at heart, and that is true."[8] The character was neither Mary Lou nor Phoebe. This was someone entirely new.

Creech could immediately tell that the speaker in her head was a gentle soul and that her grandfather was very important to her. She wrote down the line she had heard in her head and used it as the first line of a new direction for the book she had been trying to write. Remembering her college professor's warning about boring names, Creech looked at a map of New York and found the name Salamanca. She thought it was the perfect name for her new character, whose full name ended up as Salamanca Tree Hiddle. And combining Creech's own childhood desires, the fortune from the restaurant, and the American Indian–sounding name she had concocted, Salamanca Tree Hiddle became part Native American.

Did you know...

Sharon Creech is not the only author to have received a great fortune cookie fortune that prompted or foretold a wonderful future writing career. Patricia MacLachlan, author of *Sarah, Plain and Tall*, which won the 1986 Newbery Medal, once received a fortune cookie that said, "Your talents will soon be recognized." Lois Lowry, the author of two Newbery-winning novels, *Number the Stars* (1990) and *The Giver* (1994), also got a prediction from a fortune cookie, which told her that she would become rich in a far-out profession.

Creech recalled, "I didn't have the vaguest idea what her story was when I began. I just liked her voice, and I followed her along. Each day, when I'd re-read the story from the beginning, I'd pick up a new 'clue,' and then I'd follow that thread."[9] Salamanca was leading Creech on a journey that retraced the heroine's mother's final adventure.

The same stubbornness that had allowed Creech to fight for the TASIS job now made her combine Salamanca's story with the earlier story she had been working on, the one that included Mary Lou and Phoebe. After many drafts, she was able to weave the threads of each of the three girls into a beautiful story. She called it *Walk Two Moons* after the proverb in her fortune cookie. It follows Salamanca, who is called Sal for short, and her grandparents on their journey to Idaho to figure out what happened to Sal's mother. Phoebe's story comes in as Sal tells her grandparents about her friend and the struggles that she had with her own family.

"As soon as I read it, I knew it was special,"[10] said Lyle Rigg of his wife's new story. He was not the only one who thought so. Pan Macmillan accepted the manuscript, and so did HarperCollins, a publisher in the United States. Creech ended up working on the book with two editors, one from each of the publishing houses, at the same time. This was difficult for Creech, and to further complicate matters, three of the editors at HarperCollins she started out working with left, and Creech ended up with a fourth, named Joanna Cotler. The pairing turned out to be fate, as Cotler and Creech have continued to work together throughout her career.

Walk Two Moons did not get stellar reviews upon its publication in 1994. A critic for *Kirkus Reviews* remarked: "Sal's poignant story would have been stronger without quite so many remarkable coincidences or such a tidy sum of epiphanies at the end. Still, its revelations make it a fine yarn."[11] Other critics also wrote mixed reviews, expressing doubt that many children would relate to the characters, while still agreeing that the story itself was a good one.

Despite the mixed reviews, there were many who felt that Creech's book was worthy of acclaim, and Creech was about to find out how far her words were going to take her.

Patrons gather at the Book Expo America convention in New York on June 1, 2007. At this trade show, book publishers are able to show off their newest books and all of their award-winning titles.

5

Suddenly Famous

SHARON CREECH HAD found success with writing and publishing the American and British versions of *Walk Two Moons*. She immediately began to work on her next book, which would become *Chasing Redbird*. One afternoon, Creech was at home working alone. Her husband was in the United States recruiting new teachers for the school. That day, her work was proving to be particularly frustrating. She went outside to take a break and to release a muffled scream—muffled because she was the headmaster's wife, and a full-blown scream would not have been seemly. Just then, the phone rang and Creech returned inside to answer it. Expecting it to be for her husband and about school business, she grabbed a pen and paper to take a message. But rather than a note about the school, Creech wrote the words *American Library Association* and *Newbery Med*. She ended there, she says in her Newbery speech, as what the caller was saying finally sunk in. "I still go weak when I think of that call coming so unexpectedly, jolting my world so intensely,"[1] Creech recalled to the librarians gathered at the Newbery award ceremony in 1995. She felt as if God had looked down on her.

But at first, Creech barely knew what the Newbery Medal meant. She had spent most of her time teaching teens in Europe, and she had only just figured out that there was such a thing as specialized books for young adults, so she knew very little about the awards that were available for them in the United States. After she got off the phone with the Newbery committee, she received a call from an editorial assistant at her American publisher offering congratulations. Still baffled by the call and without a clue as to what the award even was, Creech asked how many of the gold medals were given out each year. "500? 100?" The assistant on the other end of the line said, "Um, Sharon, ONE. One medal."[2]

"What happens with the Newbery is a golden door opens. It creates an audience for you, because everyone hears that the book exists and it's gotten this sort of seal of approval," Creech said. But the attention generated by her Newbery win was something that was difficult for her to deal with. Creech admits to feeling "shattered for a year" from the attention. "I did nothing but answer the phone for six months," she said, "and people would call and ask if I could do IRA, ALA, BEA, and I would think, What are you talking about? What do those things mean? I had no clue. I had a cheat sheet for months."[3] The IRA, ALA,

The Newbery Medal is presented annually to the author of the most distinguished contribution to American literature for children by the Association for Library Service to Children, a division of the American Library Association (ALA). Winning the award changed the direction of Sharon Creech's career.

and BEA are professional organizations that hold conferences about reader education and books. IRA, the International Reading Association, is an organization that tries to improve reading instruction. They also put out professional journals, like *The Reading Teacher*. BEA, or BookExpo

America, is a trade show where publishers can show off their newest books and all of their award-winning titles. ALA is the American Library Association, which works to promote reading through libraries and awards excellence in books. They oversee many book awards, including the Newbery Medal. And all of these organizations wanted to help Creech celebrate her success.

In the days that followed the initial call, Creech kept expecting someone to call back and say they had made a mistake, that her book had not been awarded the highest accolade for an American book for young people. She said she did not understand why she had received such good fortune or why her book had been chosen. She admitted that she never dreamed of being given such an award. Prior to that, her biggest dream was that the books she wrote would be published, and that readers would find them, and that she could continue to write. Now, as a winner of the Newbery, she had had those dreams—and far more—answered. Creech was no longer a virtually unknown writer. People would know her name and her books and would seek her out. She would never again have to worry about whether she would be able to continue to write. She was now expected to do so.

In the busy days that followed, it was a good thing that Creech was nearly done with her next manuscript. She would need to devote all of her time over the next three months to writing her Newbery acceptance speech, which she would deliver to the Newbery Committee at the American Library Association's annual conference in June 1995.

HarperCollins republished her first book for young adults, *Absolutely Normal Chaos*, the same year that she was awarded the Newbery. American readers were eager to see more from the writer whose work was previously unknown. Now, five years after its initial publication, Creech's first book for young readers and its heroine, Mary Lou Finney, were finding an entirely new audience. After Creech delivered her acceptance speech to the ALA, she returned to writing *Chasing Redbird* and answering the constantly ringing phone. She soon realized that the demands of her new career conflicted with the one she already had.

"Our students will be losing a first-rate teacher,"[4] Lyle Rigg said in his piece for *The Horn Book Magazine* about his wife's Newbery award. Although Creech took some time off from teaching after the award was given out, it became clear that the kind of time commitment her writing life required post-Newbery would not allow her to keep teaching. Creech became a full-time writer.

Did you know...

Lyle Rigg was away on business when Sharon Creech received the call about winning the Newbery. But before he left, he had hidden a Valentine's Day present for his wife in the house. Two weeks after the Newbery call, on Valentine's Day, Rigg called Creech and revealed the location of his hidden gift. It was a miniature enameled egg. On it were paintings of the phases of the moon and around the top were the words, "May all your dreams come true."*

* Lyle D. Rigg, "Sharon Creech." *The Horn Book Magazine* Volume 71, Issue 4 (1995): p. 429.

HEADING HOME

Creech returned to *Chasing Redbird*, the manuscript she had been working on when she received the Newbery call, but her next novel to be published was *Pleasing the Ghost* in 1996. This latter book about a nine-year-old boy named Dennis follows his relationship with the ghost of his Uncle Arvie, who was named after Creech's father, Arvel. The ghost was inspired by the way Creech's father spoke following his stroke. "I had this notion that I wanted to write a funny ghost story,"[5] Creech said. She did not like scary stories and was dismayed at the kind of violence and horror often depicted in children's literature. And at the time she started writing it, she was teaching *Hamlet*, the Shakespeare play in which the title character's father appears as a ghost. After she and her students debated why a ghost would appear to someone, they concluded that the characters had unfinished business. That idea translated into *Pleasing the*

Did you know...

The year that *Walk Two Moons* was awarded the Newbery, 1995, was a great one for first-time authors and illustrators. Nancy Farmer's debut novel, *The Ear, The Eye and The Arm*, was named a Newbery honor book. Karen Cushman's debut novel, *Catherine, Called Birdy*, was also listed as a Newbery honor. Newbery honor books are those that were runners-up to winning the medal. In the children's picture book arena, first-time illustrator David Diaz won the Caldecott Medal for *Smoky Night*.

Ghost, as Uncle Arvie gets his nephew to perform three tasks for him.

A year after *Pleasing the Ghost*, Creech and Harper-Collins published *Chasing Redbird* in 1997. In it, 13-year-old Zinny, Salamanca Tree Hiddle's friend, deals with the death of her aunt at her home near the fictional town of Bybanks, Kentucky. Zinny clears brush while her uncle Nate tries to recapture his wife, whom he calls his Redbird. As she wrote the novel, death was weighing heavily on Creech, who was dealing with it in her own life.

Creech once joked to her mother that she would write about her mother's side of the family after her mother was gone. All of her stories had involved her father's side of the family and none on her mother's Italian side. But when she started writing *Bloomability* (1998), she gave the main character an Italian grandmother and dedicated the book to her mother. She even took the novel's galleys, which are the layout of the book before it is bound, to her mother. Then, as she recalled, "I was happily flying home with a copy of the galleys in my bag to show her, and she died that day, before I could put the book in her hands. It was so sad."[6]

In addition to Creech's mother's death, the year 1997 brought other profound changes. After 18 years of being a full-time teacher, and nearly 20 of living abroad, Creech and her husband were ready to come back to the United States so they could be closer to their children. In 1998, Rigg was offered a position in New Jersey as the head-master of the Pennington School, and the couple returned home.

Rigg's new job would eventually inspire Creech to write for even younger kids. Her 2001 picture book, *A Fine, Fine*

School, follows the woes of a young student whose principal is so enthusiastic about school that he decides to have it on weekends and holidays. The students' backpacks get so heavy and all of them so weary that the main character has to remind him that there are other things young kids need to learn, like climbing trees.

Over the years, Creech had become used to attending school functions with Rigg and taking on the role of the headmaster's wife. Now their roles were changing. Rigg accompanied Creech to her writing events and had to become used to people referring to him as "Mr. Creech." As Creech built her career and Rigg continued with his, they found harmony working out of their new home, a red-brick building on the campus of the Pennington School in New Jersey. There, Creech continued to pen stories with the kind of writing that many had already fallen in love with.

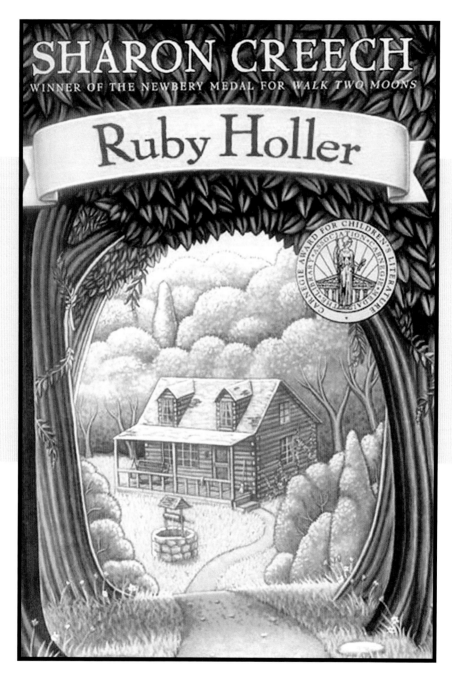

Sharon Creech earned the Carnegie Medal for her magical-realism novel, Ruby Holler. A letter she received from her aunt, which described her father's impish ways as a youngster, had inspired the book.

6

Creech's Beloved Books

WHY HAVE SHARON CREECH'S books so often met with critical and popular success? Part of the reason may be because of her ability to describe out-of-the-ordinary characters in extraordinary situations, as well as her desire to give her readers an opportunity to learn. Creech quickly became a favorite of students and teachers alike, because her books are filled with the kinds of teachable moments that not only round out her characters, but could also help round out a curriculum.

A fine example of this can be found in *Absolutely Normal Chaos*, in her depiction of Mary Lou Finney, the protagonist. In it, Creech employs journaling, a device she used with her students and decided to try out for herself. "Through her depiction of Mary Lou as an enthusiastic teen . . . Creech develops a spunky character that teen readers are eager to know, one they are likely to want to befriend,"[1] wrote Pamela Sissi Carroll in her book *Sharon Creech: Teen Reads: Student Companions to Young Adult Literature.* In the same novel, Creech also added a literature lesson. As Mary Lou reads Homer's *The Odyssey*, she finds herself learning something about the human condition. When Circe turns the men into pigs in the epic poem, Mary Lou learns it is a metaphor about real life. "Women turn men into pigs all the time,"[2] her cousin humorously tells her. It is a lesson, no doubt, that former teacher Creech enjoyed pointing out to her readers.

Her memories also inspired much of this novel. Creech has said she was remembering her family life growing up as she wrote it, even giving Mary Lou her old address at 4059 Buxton Road. Another memory from her youth inspired her next book for children, *Walk Two Moons.* When Creech came across the fortune cookie with the Native American proverb, the kid in her probably could not resist the connection with her childhood desire to be Native American, just as the teacher in her could not resist using the lesson about not judging someone until you had walked in his or her moccasins for a while. She compounded the lesson with one that would help students better understand a classic literary structure: the journey.

"*Walk Two Moons* extends the story within the story. In a time-honored tradition it tells of a trip, a pilgrimage of sorts. During the journey, thirteen-year-old Sal diverts her grandparents with the story of her friend Phoebe, a tale that tangles with her own," says Newbery-winning author Richard Peck, adding that the book "invites a deeper understanding of the adult world, and this story of a search for the mother challenges the young reader whose goal is to avoid her own."[3] In the *Journal of Reading*, a reviewer wrote, "This story of adolescent growth and awareness is absorbing to its bittersweet ending."[4] Yet some reviewers just did not get Sal's story. "*School Library Journal* praises its 'humor and suspense,' if you're in the mood for humor about a mother's death,"[5] said Hal Piper, writing for the *Chicago Tribune.* Piper believed that too many children's books had these heavy plots.

Creech's next book, *Pleasing the Ghost*, was also criticized for making light of a serious issue, this time speech impediments. Creech used the pattern of her father's speech to create the miscommunications of Uncle Arvie (also named after her father) in *Pleasing the Ghost.* She recalled, "My father, Arvel, had a stroke, which left him unable to speak correctly. Sometimes the sounds and words that came out of his mouth were both funny (their sounds) and sad (because he couldn't say what he meant)."[6] Reviews of the book were mixed. "Simultaneously sensitive and ridiculous," said two *Publishers Weekly* reviewers, "Creech's attention to nuances of feeling grounds this light tale in emotional truth."[7] Mary Jo Drungil, reviewing the book for *School Library Journal*, felt differently and called it "a disappointing tale." She went on to argue, "Arvie's nonsense syllables seem exaggerated to the point of caricature, thus creating an offensive effect."[8]

Creech's next book, *Chasing Redbird*, was not quite as controversial. "As I was writing, I was vaguely aware that the trail was working on many levels," Creech recalled in describing the trails that her main character, Zinny, uncovers in the novel. "Not only was it a real, literal trail in the woods, but it also seemed to mirror the trails we all follow in our lives (Which way should we go? What should we do?) and also to mirror the writing process (Which way will this story turn? Why can't I see where it's going?)"[9] For a literature teacher, the layers may have been hard to resist.

Creech received high marks for her work. "Creech masterfully creates characters and almost surreal, yet totally plausible situations to engage readers and listeners with stories that will linger long after the final line,"[10] said Susan McCaffrey. Reporting for *The Reading Teacher*, Pamela J. Dunston wrote in agreement, "Zinny embarks on a journey of self-discovery and learns that the mysteries of the trail are connected to long-kept family secrets."[11] She also advised teachers to use the book as a springboard to map-reading or wilderness survival and emergency medicine activities. *New York Times* reviewer Ethel Heins, writing for *The Horn Book Magazine*, called *Chasing Redbird* "a striking novel, notable for its emotional honesty. . . . The writing is laced with figurative language and folksy comments that intensify both atmosphere and emotion."[12] Creech herself found the novel a pleasure. She remarked, "One of the most enjoyable parts about writing this book was coming up with my own names for places along Zinny's trail, like Baby Toe Ridge and Donut Hole and Hogback Hill."[13]

Switzerland, another interesting location, inspired *Bloomability*, Creech's next novel. In it, she sought to capture the feelings she and her family had experienced when they lived in Switzerland for two years. Creech, a somewhat shy author, is unusually revealing of herself on the cover of this book. The artist renderings of photos, which appear on the cover of the first-edition hardcover, are based on actual photos of Creech's family. The largest photo is of her daughter, Karin, on top of a mountain. A picture of her youngest brother, Tom, is beneath it, and to the right of that is the house the family lived in during their stay in Switzerland. The back of the book also has pictures of her children in another Swiss town and a picture of her husband.

The book was called *Bloomability* because of the way one of the main character's classmates mispronounced "possibility" in the book. Dinnie, the protagonist, is kidnapped by an aunt and uncle and taken to a boarding school in Switzerland to get away from her father, who moves all over the place; her jailed older brother; and her pregnant 16-year-old sister.

Though her fans devoured Creech's latest novel, *Bloomability* received somewhat negative reviews. One review complained, "Fans of the author's previous works will

Did you know...

According to the Association for Library Service to Children (ALSC), a division of the American Library Association, *Walk Two Moons* has been translated into a number of other languages. In Denmark, it was translated into Danish and it is called *Målt med evigheden* (*Measured with Eternity*). In Italy, it is *Due Lune* (*Two Moons*). In Spanish-speaking countries, it has been translated and sold under two different titles, *Caminar Dos Lunas* (*Walk Two Moons*) and *Entre Dos Lunas* (*Between Two Moons*).

likely miss her more fully realized characters."[14] Nancy Bond agreed, writing, "Dinnie's attachment to and home-sickness for [her family] is talked about rather than truly felt, and her two aunts, Grace and Tillie, with their repeated postcard messages, become tiresome."[15]

INSPIRED BY FAMILY AND POETRY

"I felt like such a wanderer, endlessly roaming, yearning for home,"[16] Creech says of 1997, the tumultuous year before she returned to live in America. Her mother's illness and eventual death and her husband's search for a job in the United States had the family crossing the Atlantic between the United States and England a total of 12 times. Then, when her daughter Karin took a transatlantic boat trip and said that she nearly died in a gale before arriving safely in Ireland, Creech's next novel, *The Wanderer*, was born.

Critics did not know what to make of *The Wanderer*. "The novel is rather too obviously a voyage of self-discovery, with the ocean metaphor equally spelled out,"[17] wrote Roger Sutton for *The Horn Book Magazine.* Reviewer Angela Schult felt differently, saying, "After reading this book, I was reminded of why Sharon Creech is one of my favorite authors."[18] Although *The Wanderer* got mixed reviews, it garnered eight awards, including a Newbery Honor.

Fishing in the Air, Creech's first picture book, was also based on experiences with her father, a frequent source of inspiration. She remembers fishing trips with her father and what he taught her and her siblings about enjoying the outdoors. As she wrote the book, she came to the realiza-tion that fishing is not about catching the fish, but about casting your line into the air. In true Creech form, she reached back into a previous book to pull pieces for this one. In *Walk Two Moons*, Sal calls herself a "fisher in the air." Creech said that for this picture book she was trying to illustrate how parents give their children the gift of imagination. But not all of Creech's gifts of imagination came from her parents. Her next title would be inspired by someone who was nearly a stranger to her.

Creech was not trying to experiment with new formats when she decided on her next title, *Love That Dog*. She was not even sure it was a book when she had finished writing it, but after her editor, Joanna Cotler, got a look at it, she assured Creech it was indeed a book, and a good one at that.

Creech's work had been inspired by the Walter Dean Myers poem, "Love That Boy." The first stanza of the poem was in a card that her friend, librarian K.T. Horning of the Cooperative Children's Book Center, had given her. Creech put it on her bulletin board and looked at it every day for years. Then one day she wondered about the boy in Myers's poem and whom he might love. Instantly, her character Jack appeared. Because the poem was the impetus for her writing, her book also came out in verse. Creech was surprised to find that she had written the poet Walter Dean Myers into her book. She told her editor that she would not want the book published if Myers was in any way uncomfortable with his appearance in her fiction. Fortunately, Myers (who Creech had met only once before) did not mind.

Creech's experiment was a successful one among critics. A reviewer for the *New York Times* said, "*Love That Dog* isn't only a memorable book, it's also a needed one."[19] Creech taps into her former teacher and shows, through Jack's poems, how his teacher influences the way he thinks about poetry; he then uses poetry to express himself. "Jack's poems are immediate and powerful, and after hearing them, children will be inspired to try writing their own,"[20] remarked Laura Tillotson for *Book Links*. Interestingly, although this was Creech's seventh title, the year it was published she was awarded by U.S. booksellers a *Publishers Weekly* "off-the-cuff" award, called The Cuffies, for "Most Promising New Author."

Creech was inspired next by her husband, and his job as headmaster, for her second picture book, *A Fine, Fine School*. It is the story of Tillie, who goes to a school with a well-meaning but overzealous headmaster. Trouble arises when the headmaster starts to have school on weekends and holidays, and yet Tillie's little brother has not learned how to climb a tree because Tillie is too busy at school to teach him. Tillie reminds the principal that there is more to life than books. Of the picture book, one critic wrote, "This delightful, amusing picture book is a wonderful tribute to all those principals and teachers who passionately care about their students' learning. At the same time, it serves as a good reminder that the best kinds of life learning often take place outside of the classroom walls."[21] Like many of Creech's titles, this one turned out to be particularly popular with educators.

Creech's aunt provided the material for her next novel: a story in a letter. Six years before *Ruby Holler* was published, the author got a letter from her aunt, which told a story about Creech's mischievous father. It ended, "And that was when we lived in the holler." Creech immediately imagined an enchanting location and was intrigued with the thought of her family living in such a place, so she used the setting for the story of orphans Dallas and Florida. After beginning to write the novel, she saw a photo of the house her father had lived in, which was no better than a shack. A disappointed Creech was glad she had not seen the picture first, or it would have ruined the picture in her imagination, as well as in her book. Of the book, she remarked:

> What I want children to get out of *Ruby Holler* is whatever they want. It is just a story, there is no message. I never start with 'I'm going to tell a story that proves that old people help younger people'—but it's something at the back of my mind that I must be plumbing because it's kind of in every book.[22]

After its publication, *Ruby Holler* went on to win the Carnegie Medal, which is the United Kingdom's equivalent of the Newbery Medal. Creech—who had previously been shortlisted for the award for both *The Wanderer* and *Love That Dog*—had now become the first American to win the medal. It further underscored her status as a children's writer of dependable excellence, admired both in her native country and abroad. Yet she was distressed that the Carnegie Medal was not taken advantage of like the Newbery was in the United States. "When I was in the UK after receiving the Newbery, there was very little understanding of that or capitalizing on it," she said after her Carnegie win. Anne Marley, part of the Carnegie judging panel, agreed: "Booksellers are missing a great opportunity in not getting behind [the award]. Parents are desperate for recommendations of good books, and that is exactly what the Carnegie shortlist provides."[23]

GRANDPARENTHOOD

Now with grown children, Creech knew the next phase of her life was fast approaching—becoming a grandmother. In her next books, as this idea became a certainty, Creech focused more on the relationships between grandparents and their grandchildren. Although she had written about grandparents before, books like Creech's next title, *Granny Torrelli Makes Soup*, were the first she would produce as a grandparent herself.

"There is something juicy and rich about Creech's writing," wrote reviewer Traci Todd about *Granny Torrelli Makes Soup*. "In her hands, soup making, for example, becomes less about stock and noodles and more about living a rich and flavorful life."[24] Creech began writing this story after she heard that her daughter was expecting

Did you know...

The Carnegie Medal, established in Great Britain in 1936, is the oldest children's book award, though it has only recently begun to receive media attention. It was set up in memory of businessman and philanthropist Andrew Carnegie, who established more than 2,800 libraries around the world. The award recognizes quality in children's literature and is decided on by a panel of judges from the Chartered Institute of Library and Information Professionals (CILIP). Other winners have included such acclaimed authors as C.S. Lewis and Philip Pullman. The other major UK award is the Kate Greenaway Prize, which is similar to the Caldecott Medal in the United States. It recognizes excellence in picture book illustrations.

her first child and Creech thought about being a first-time grandmother: "It seemed that most of my memories of my grandmothers swirled around kitchens and food."[25] In this story, Granny Torrelli, patterned after Creech's Italian grandmother, makes *zuppa*—soup—in the kitchen and cooks up the bonds of friendship with the spices. In her review, Karen Coats writes that the story "has genuine warmth and affection."[26]

There is another grandparent at the center of Creech's book *Heartbeat*. In it, Annie's grandfather is beginning to forget things, and Annie is having trouble with the other relationships in her life as well. To pen Annie's story, Creech again turned to free-verse poetry. "The rhythm of Creech's language makes this free verse novel almost a song,"[27] said reviewers for *Language Arts*, and other reviewers agreed that verse was an excellent choice. Following *Heartbeat*'s publication, Creech was again short-listed for the Carnegie Medal.

Creech describes her next work, *Replay*, as a book "about a boy in a big Italian family, full of absolutely normal chaos."[28] Here, she comes back to another love—the theater—in this part novel, part play-within-a-play. In classic form, Creech manages to weave several different threads together to form a seamless story. The book was inspired in part by her granddaughter Pearl, who has a wonderful imagination and tells interesting stories, including one where Pearl cast herself in the role of an angel (Creech would use this as the impetus for a later book). The character of Leo therefore came out of the idea of the creative Pearl—he is also someone who retells the events in his life a little differently. The author offered, "And maybe that is what I am trying to do in each book I write. Offer readers

SHARON CREECH

WINNER OF THE NEWBERY MEDAL FOR *WALK TWO MOONS*

heartbeat

As an author, Sharon Creech has always sought new challenges for herself. Her 2004 book Heartbeat, *about the adventures of a girl named Annie, is written in blank verse.*

little moments that are more pleasing to their ears, eyes, minds. Moments which might replace other more drab or hurtful ones they encounter in the real world."[29]

"I've also finished a picture book of new baby songs, poems from the perspective of a new baby. These were written shortly after my granddaughter was born."[30] The book, titled *Who's That Baby?*, was Creech's third picture book. She started it as a Christmas gift to her granddaughter Pearl, and she originally wanted it simply to be a collection of poems and songs that accompanied Pearl's newborn pictures. It then evolved into a publishable book. David Diaz, the book's illustrator, had won the Caldecott Medal in 1995, the same year that Creech won the Newbery. Both were virtually unknown at the time. But by the publication date of *Who's That Baby?* in 2006, both Diaz and Creech had well-established careers.

FURTHER EXPERIMENTATION

Although Creech had built her career by writing realistic characters in the present-day world, she took a departure for *The Castle Corona*, a fairy tale set in feudal Italy. The story involves a ridiculous royal family and two orphaned peasant children, all tired of their lot in life. "When I began this book, I didn't know whether it would be serious or humorous, but once I met the royals, ho! They made me laugh,"[31] says Creech on her Web site. The book was inspired by her childhood dreams of fairy-tale castles and by the many castles she saw when she lived and traveled throughout Europe.

Despite the fun Creech had writing it, the novel met with mixed reviews. "The hasty revelations at story's end don't entirely satisfy,"[32] said Jennifer Mattson writing for

Booklist. Another reviewer agreed that "it's disappointing that after over 300 pages the ending contains no real surprises," but did find that Creech "weaves her many characters into a delicate tapestry."[33] Karen Coats, however, called the book "an easy sell" to those who loved fairy tales, and called Creech's writing "graceful."[34]

For her next book, Creech wrote *Hate That Cat*, which was a sequel to the fan favorite and her first experiment in writing in verse, *Love That Dog.* It is a year later for Jack and Miss Stretchberry, and the reluctance Jack felt about writing is gone. He now pours out his feelings about his relationship with his mother and a brand-new kitten. "*Hate That Cat* extends Creech's attempts to make poetry something that children can appreciate as part of daily life,"[35] wrote Susan Dove Lempke for *The Horn Book Magazine.* Thom Barthelmess called it a "worthy companion"[36] to the original.

Creech and Rigg returned to Switzerland for the 2007–2008 school year. Upon arriving, Creech was inspired by her new surroundings. The tower on the school's campus became part of the setting for her next book, *The Unfinished Angel.* Another inspiration for the book came from a story that Creech's granddaughter had made up as a two-year-old: "Once upon a time in Spain, there was an angel, and that angel was me." The tower would serve as the home for her book's angel, and the town around it and all the people who lived there, the characters. And the angel's stilted speech was inspired by Creech's own frustrations to learn Italian, when both English and Italian got mixed up in her head and she was speaking neither language very well.

Critics and fans alike were united in their praise for *The Unfinished Angel.* A reviewer for the *Wall Street Journal* called the novel "unbelievably sweet"[37] and readers on the Web site Library Thing ranged from calling it "a simple and beautiful book about compassion" to "hilarious."[38]

Actress Abigail Breslin poses for photos at the Bally's in Las Vegas on March 13, 2008. After being nominated for an Academy Award, the young actress bought the rights to film Sharon Creech's novel Ruby Holler.

7

Print, Stage, and Film

SINCE WINNING THE Newbery, Sharon Creech has continued to publish books of high caliber at a nearly breakneck speed—not to mention ones that have become well-loved by students, teachers, and many other readers. In 15 years, 16 of her books have amassed dozens of awards and accolades and have earned Creech the position of fan favorite. Although Creech gained instant popularity with her Newbery win for her second book for young adults, the millennium opened up more opportunities for her to reach far more readers with new formats, collaborations, and even a different publishing house.

Although Creech had experimented with different written formats, she had never explored magazine writing. In 2004, the editors of *New Moon*, a small Minnesota-based magazine, partnered with HarperCollins in an effort to promote Creech and her books. The magazine had gotten its start in 1996 when Nancy Gruver was inspired by her 11-year-old twin girls to publish a magazine that was created by girls, for girls. The magazine has no ads, and the online content is strictly moderated. Since its first inception, the magazine has won many awards, including Parents' Choice Foundation awards. The magazine featured a Sharon Creech book club and gave its readers the first opportunity to read *Heartbeat* before the book was published. Josette Jurey, senior manager of publicity for HarperCollins Children's Books, said at the time, "It's very rare that we sell serial rights on middle-grade novels. In fact, this is the first time we've done it. I don't know of anyone else doing this kind of collaboration with middle-grade novels."[1] (Serial rights are the rights to print a book in a magazine. The book is broken up into chapters or shorter pieces that appear in order in several issues.) While today the magazine, which is now called *New Moon Girls*, no longer has a Sharon Creech book club, the partnership proved profitable for the time it endured.

THE PLAY'S THE THING

Creech's first American novel, *Walk Two Moons*, was deemed popular enough to translate into a stage play in 2005. The theater company TheatreWorks/USA (formerly TheatreWorks/NYC) adapted the book into a play with an eye to family entertainment, like other successful Broadway shows such as *The Lion King*. TheatreWorks/USA began in 1961 and has toured all over the country performing children's theater. The company was used to touring nationwide and doing shows that ran for a minimum number of times—as few as two performances in some towns, while sometimes for two weeks in larger cities. Performing in one place—the Lucille Lortel Theater in Manhattan—for a run of two months was a big risk for the theater, but the company was buoyed by the thought that Creech's novel was so well written and so well loved that it would translate into a large box office take. The theater group had cut its teeth on other literary blockbusters like *Sarah, Plain and Tall*; *Charlotte's Web*; and the Junie B. Jones series, and believed that *Walk Two Moons* could withstand the two-month run in New York City.

Artistic director Barbara Pasternack felt that the shift from being a traveling company to one with a defined home was necessary for TheatreWorks. As school curriculum guidelines became more specific, Pasternack felt that teachers needed to know what benchmarks the play would cover so that they could justify attending. "Now everything has to be curriculum-oriented, right on the nose for teachers of kids in the community you serve out there," she said. "We sell what we make and that's great, but when you have to sell everything you make and that starts to define your art, you can't ever take a risk."[2]

Unlike TheatreWorks, Creech never had to worry about such burdens as fitting into a specific curriculum. In fact, she made sure to say that she wrote *Ruby Holler* just so children could enjoy it, not to make any specific point about anything. As Creech's career went on, though, and as she appeared more and more on summer recommended reading lists, she found herself butting up against detractors who felt, like the creators at TheatreWorks, that the demands of curriculum were beginning to outweigh the enjoyment and creation of art.

After the success of *Replay*, Creech tried her hand at creating a work specifically for student theater. The play collection *Acting Out!* was editor Justin Chanda's idea: to bring together Newbery-winning authors to write plays for children. (*Acting Out!* was published by Simon & Schuster. It was the only time that a Creech book was done outside of HarperCollins and with an editor other than Joanna Cotler.) Six Newbery "stars" would participate in the book—Avi, Susan Cooper, Patricia MacLachlan, Katherine Paterson, Richard Peck, and Creech—all without restrictions, except for one rule. Chanda said, "I asked each playwright to choose one word. It could have been a favorite word, a goofy word, or even a word they thought might stump the other playwrights. They were allowed to use the words in any way they wanted, but each of the six words had to appear somewhere in their script."[3] The chosen words were: *Dollop*, *hoodwink*, *Justin*, *knuckleball*,

---

Did you know...

The first children's book that TheatreWorks/USA turned into a play was *Harold and the Purple Crayon*. Though the company started by doing shows about historical figures like Abraham Lincoln, they found that optioning children's books and making them into plays was a great way to engage students and teachers.

panhandle, and *raven*. Creech's word was *raven*, which was also the title of her play in the book. Inspired by the creature in Edgar Allan Poe's poem "The Raven," her play concerns a young Poe, age 12, who is being encouraged by a New York book editor to lighten up his classically dark poem.

Reviews for the book and its plays were good, except for the play by Avi and the one penned by MacLachlan, which one reviewer believed "falls flat."[4] A Wisconsin school librarian, who had no issues with any of the plays, said, "The plays beg to be acted out; silent reading does not do the book justice."[5] Some of her fifth grade students performed one of the plays with great enthusiasm, as she imagined the playwrights would have intended.

AND . . . ACTION!

The people behind TheatreWorks were not the only ones who thought that Creech's stories would translate nicely into other formats. In 2007, after young actress Abigail Breslin was nominated for an Academy Award for her portrayal of Olive in the movie *Little Miss Sunshine*, she bought the movie option to *Ruby Holler*. Breslin may have been attracted to the story of another unusual yet loving family, like the one that was portrayed in *Little Miss Sunshine*. This was the third set of movie rights that Creech was able to sell. Prior to Breslin's buy, Teri Hatcher, who stars on the television show *Desperate Housewives*, had bought the movie rights to *Bloomability*, and Creech's agent had sold the rights to *Walk Two Moons* to the production company Rocket Dreams nearly a year before that. Though the movie options have been bought, none of Creech's works have made it to film screens . . . at least, not yet.

Sharon Creech continues to find inspiration in writing for young people. She believes it is important to address often-difficult issues that children face with humor and grace.

8

Words She Says

WHERE DOES SHARON CREECH find her inspiration? How does she turn that inspiration into a publishable book? She once said:

> A book usually begins with a very clear image in my mind of a person and a place. These images come unbidden; they're always a surprise. Sometimes this person and place will hover there for days, weeks, months, until I also hear the person's voice. As soon as I hear the voice (usually it's one sentence or a phrase), I feel compelled to begin "recording" that voice, to explore the place, to find out what this character is up to.[1]

Creech has described an ideal writing day for her as being in the office by 8:30 A.M.: "I usually write in the mornings and evenings for two or three hours at a time, but when I'm exploring a first draft, I write all day long and into the night and wander around like a zombie, living in the world of the book."[2] She then reads and answers e-mails for an hour before she gets on with writing, which she does directly on her computer. She starts by revising everything that she wrote the day before. Sometimes the revisions are small, but sometimes they involve cutting whole scenes. She thinks that by the time she has completed a first draft, she has probably revised every page a few dozen times.

Creech never worries about writer's block. "I've always thought that there were too many ideas and not enough time to sit down and develop them,"[3] she has said. She never really knows where her books are heading when she starts working on a new story—and therefore spends a lot of her writing time exploring the ideas and clues that her protagonists give her. She says that writers need to have a lot of patience in order to uncover the layers and layers that are in each of their characters, because after doing the work, they will eventually find gold.

"I use pastel colored paper for manuscript drafts," Creech says on her blog. "The colors help my memory. If I need to quickly refer back to an incident, I can remember when I wrote that scene and what color paper it is on, and I can find it easily." She says that final drafts are "white and pristine."[4] After a first draft is finished, Creech leaves it alone for a few weeks, and then comes back to it to do another round of edits, which she writes longhand on a printout of the manuscript. When she has written so much that she can barely read it anymore, she starts typing the second draft. After another round of edits and a third draft, she sends it off to her editor.

Although Creech has made awards lists with every book she has written except for her one unpublished one, she still worries that her editor will tell her that what she has written is trash. Fortunately, her editor has never thought that. Cotler returns comments to Creech, and the author then works on perhaps two more full drafts. She works until she feels that she cannot change another word.

"A book contains hundreds, maybe thousands, of ideas, squirming and changing and evolving as I write,"[5] she notes. But Creech cannot reveal all of the places from which she culls the seeds of her stories. "I hope to leave some of it a mystery—even to myself,"[6] she said in her Newbery speech for *Walk Two Moons*. Perhaps it is best not to know all the elements that are woven into a book, or it may spoil some of its magic. Many of those squirming ideas remain with Creech as loose threads after she has finished one book. Although Creech does not usually write sequels, many of the ideas and elements of one story crop up again in others. In the case of Jack in *Love That Dog*, for example, it was Jack's voice that remained as a loose thread, so Creech picked it up again and followed him into the next year of school to write *Hate That Cat*.

When Creech begins writing, she is very much aware of the age of her main character: "If it's a 13-year-old girl, I try to write exactly from the consciousness of a 13-year-old girl. If it's a 9-year-old boy, then I try to be in the mind of a 9-year-old boy. If I'm faithful to that, then I know that the story will work."[7] Yet Creech is unsure as to why her books have such appeal to people of all ages. She describes seeing grandparents, children, and adults buying her books for themselves. She finds it interesting that they have all found something in her stories. Creech never tries to classify her books. "I know that publishers have to classify books, say, as Children's or Young Adult or Adult, in order to better market them,"[8] Creech said, but she thinks that books are books, only many of hers have young people in the main role.

WORDS OF ADVICE

For aspiring writers, Creech offers the same advice that many may have heard before, but she believes that it is still the best advice she could give: "It's simple, but valid: read a lot and write a lot. The more you read, the more you are exposed to techniques of characterization, dialogue, plot, etc. The more you write, the stronger your writing 'muscles' become and the easier it becomes to hear your own voice."[9]

She once commented that the only difference in choosing to write for adults or for children is the age of the protagonist, and that it is just common sense. She has also said that it is important for new writers "to know how to use words well, to think creatively, to understand plot, character, theme, tone, to know how to tell a story."[10] Then it would not matter if they were writing for children or adults. Though Creech admits that writing is a lengthy process, she knows firsthand that it gets better as you go along: "It takes less time now to produce a novel than it used to, and I think that is because I'm able to avoid some of the pitfalls of early attempts. I've learned something!" Yet she admits that this is not always the case. "I took several wrong turns with both *Ruby Holler* and with *Replay*, and those books seemed to take eons to complete."[11]

On the mechanics of writing, though, Creech offers what reads like a recipe:

> Read a lot, live your life, and listen and watch, so that your mind fills up with millions of images. Shake it. See what floats to the top. Transfer floating images to page, word by word. Repeat. When it is all done, remove clunky bits. Sounds simple, yes? And it is, if you stay loose and open, and if you have the patience to transfer those images, word by word, from your mind to the paper.[12]

Ultimately, though, Creech thinks that writers shouldn't take too much advice from others. She says they need to listen to themselves, or they will end up sounding like everyone else. "You can listen to all the advice, but you need to tailor it to your own imagination jungle."[13]

FANS

Of course, not all of Creech's days are spent writing. However long it takes her to complete her work, there are a vast number of admirers who eagerly await her next offering, and many of them are in schools, a place very familiar to the former teacher. She could spend an entire day reading and responding to the fan mail that she gets every week. "I figured out one time how long it takes. It's something like nine minutes to read a letter, write a note, and address and stamp the envelope,"[14] she told an interviewer. Though it is time-consuming, Creech prefers to read her mail herself, rather than have an assistant do it. Creech also makes speeches and visits schools. Although she was a teacher, she finds it difficult to approach her own books as materials for instruction; it is much easier for her to teach someone else's book rather than one of her own.

One of Sharon Creech's favorite authors is the poet and novelist *Rainer Maria Rilke*, seen here circa 1906, who is one of the most important writers in the German language. The title of her blog is taken from a Rilke quote.

TEACH CREECH

Though Creech left teaching long ago, something of the teacher in her has remained, as she weaves lessons into her prose. Themes, character studies, plays, story structures, and more have been taught from the pages of her books. In that way, Creech has never really left the classroom. Creech's own Web site even welcomes teachers and helps them plan their lessons for her books with the "Teach Creech" section of the site.

The "Teach Creech" section provides teachers with downloadable documents that include instructions for teaching all of her books, with additional documents for her most recent titles. The documents offer a sample lesson for

Did you know...

Sharon Creech began her own blog in 2009. On it, you can see interviews with Creech and videos of her exploring her surroundings, including a spooky cupboard that she discovered in 2009 in the house they were staying at while her husband taught at the Switzerland TASIS school. The blog is called "Words We Say" after a quote from poet and novelist Rainer Maria Rilke, which Creech has in a sidebar on the blog. Rilke was born in Prague and lived from 1875 to 1926, but he influenced many modern artists, including J.D. Salinger, the author of *Franny and Zooey* and *The Catcher in the Rye*; Julia Alvarez, the author of *How the Garcia Girls Lost their Accents*; and even pop singer Lady Gaga.

teachers, advice on how to address each book, how to schedule time for the lessons to be implemented, and even assessment guidelines so that teachers can evaluate their students' progress.

The site employs the use of cross-curricular activities by addressing other subject areas, such as health—"Have students choose one character and research the prevention and treatment of the medical problems this character faces"—or math—"If *The Wanderer* was traveling at

Did you know...

Creech credits many writers from varying times, places, and genres for giving her inspiration. They include: Geoffrey Chaucer, the author of *The Canterbury Tales*, which she taught to her students; F. Scott Fitzgerald, who wrote *The Great Gatsby*; American novelist and short-story writer Flannery O'Connor; Charles Dickens, the author of many great works including *David Copperfield*; Cuban-born author and journalist Italo Calvino, best known for his novel *If On a Winter's Night a Traveler*; E.B. White, the author of *Charlotte's Web*; Richard Peck, whose book, *A Year Down Yonder*, won the Newbery Medal in 2001; Lois Lowry, the author of another Newbery winner, *The Giver*; Kate DiCamillo, whose novels *Because of Winn-Dixie* and *The Tale of Despereaux* were made into feature films; and Jerry Spinelli, the author of the Newbery Medal–winning *Maniac Magee*.

A circa-1925 photo of one of Sharon Creech's favorite authors, F. Scott Fitzgerald. Though best known in his lifetime as a popular short story writer, he is today highly regarded for his novels, particularly The Great Gatsby, *which is considered among the greatest novels in American literature.*

20 knots, how many miles per hour is that? (1 knot= 1.15 mph)"—or science—"Have students research the science of geysers like Old Faithful."[15] But Creech's site is not the only one that provides teaching resources for schools. Other publications have seen how teachers gravitate toward her work, and they have created their own materials. Marta Segal wrote a teaching guide for *Walk Two Moons* after it won the Newbery. She breaks down each chapter and lists discussion questions for teachers and students to follow to explore the book, such as: "Sal says her story is hidden beneath Phoebe's. What do you think she means by this?"[16] Segal also makes suggestions for using a map of the United States to track the places that the Hiddles go on their travels. She also suggests exploring the kinds of myths that appear in the book.

"A HEADACHE IN MY STOMACH"

Because schools and teachers have embraced Creech's work, the titles of her books often appear on reading lists across the country. But not everyone thinks that Creech's work deserves all the praise that has been heaped on it. Some even think that making her work required reading is a bad idea.

Barbara Feinberg, a teacher, is one of those who has criticized the kinds of books that Creech often writes. In a 2004 article in the *New York Times*, she took issue with the genre of "problem books," which involve young characters experiencing difficulties that are caused by the adults in their lives. She argued that such books did more harm than good to their readers. "The required books are often the 'good books'— that is, the ones that garner the highest literary prizes, like the Newbery Medal," she said, adding that while she agreed that many of the books are well written, "the angst and crash landings of the books is what sticks with you. A 10-year-old attending the creative arts program I run told me, 'Those books give me a headache in my stomach.'"[17]

Feinberg went on to argue that what makes a book useful to young readers is insight into themselves, but often these books are pushing insights that their readers are not quite ready for, with protagonists who have no measures by which to protect themselves. She cites other books in which the main characters deal with difficult situations, including the Harry Potter series, *The Devil's Arithmetic*, and *The Watsons Go to Birmingham—1963*, as being more beneficial to young readers. Although these novels, by J.K. Rowling, Jane Yolen, and Christopher Paul Curtis respectively, deal with the murder of the main character's parents, the Holocaust, and the racist American South, the issues are handled in a way that the main character is somewhat protected, whether by magic or the intervention of caring adults. She asserts this is a much easier way for young readers to process the harrowing elements in each book.

Feinberg says that her son did not enjoy many of Creech's books because everyone died in them. By the time Creech began writing *Bloomability*, she was quite aware of the number of deaths on the pages of her books. She remarked, "I set myself a challenge in this book early on: in this book, *no one would die!!* That's been very hard, you know? It takes a lot of energy to keep everyone alive."[18]

Another teacher wrote about similar issues in a 2007 article, which says that the level of realism in novels "has taken on a measure of hopelessness that often leaves readers wondering if there is any possibility of redemption."[19] Like Feinberg, this teacher also has other literary suggestions, like *Great Expectations* by Charles Dickens. What he likes in that Dickens novel is how the main character responds to the things that are happening around him. "I recognize in Pip a sense of magic. The world is peopled with unseen potentials even when life gets hard." The author goes on to say that "maybe this is the optimism we need to celebrate in students."[20] He suggests that teachers find other titles to round out their reading lists—books with a sense of hope.

In some ways, such opinions mark Creech's enormous influence on the children's literary scene. With so much love and praise for her work, there have to be some detractors as well. Creech's writing speaks to people on many different levels, which is probably why so many people of varying backgrounds and ages respond to her work. It is only inevitable that some should have a negative reaction.

Sharon Creech herself has no worries. After two successful, enriching careers, Creech is continuing on a path that many are happy to see her on—as an outstanding author of young adult literature. If she maintains her nearly breakneck pace of producing a book almost every year, readers will have many more Creech titles to consume in the years to come.

CHRONOLOGY

1945 Sharon Creech is born to Ann and Arvel on July 29 in Ohio.

1963 Creech graduates from Brush High School in South Euclid, Ohio.

1967 She graduates from Hiram College with a bachelor's degree in English literature; Creech marries H.R. Leuthy Jr.

1968 Creech and Leuthy have their first child, son Robert.

1971 Creech's second child is born, a girl, Karin.

1978 She receives her master's degree in English literature and writing from George Mason University in Virginia; Creech and Leuthy divorce.

1979 Creech accepts a position for TASIS and moves to England with her children.

1982 She marries Lyle Rigg. The family moves to Montagnola, Switzerland.

1984 Creech and her family return to England.

1988 She wins the Billee Murray Denny Poetry Award and $1,000 for her poem, "Cleansing."

1990 *The Recital* and *Absolutely Normal Chaos* are published in England.

1991 *Nickel Malley* is published in England.

1994 *Walk Two Moons* is published simultaneously in England and in the United States.

1995 *Walk Two Moons* wins the Newbery Medal; *Absolutely Normal Chaos* is published in the United States.

1996 *Pleasing the Ghost* is published.

1997 *Chasing Redbird* is published.

1998 *Bloomability* is published. Rigg gets a job at a school in Pennington, New Jersey; Creech and Rigg return to the United States.

2000 *The Wanderer* and *Fishing in the Air* are published.

2001 *The Wanderer* is named a Newbery Honor book; *A Fine, Fine School* and *Love That Dog* are published; *Love That Dog* wins the Claudia Lewis Poetry Award.

2002 *Ruby Holler* is published and wins the Carnegie Medal in the United Kingdom.

2003 *Granny Torrelli Makes Soup* is published.

2004 *Heartbeat* is published.

2005 *Replay* is published.

2006 *Who's That Baby?* is published.

2007 *The Castle Corona* is published; Creech and Rigg return to Switzerland for the 2007–2008 school year.

2008 *Hate That Cat* is published.

2009 Creech begins writing a blog; she and Rigg move to North Carolina; *The Unfinished Angel* is published.

NOTES

Chapter 1

1 "Sharon Creech on *Love That Dog*." Twenty by Jenny. http://www.youtube.com/watch?v=9atmYRlEzCM.

2 Sharon Creech, "Newbery Medal Acceptance." *The Horn Book Magazine*. Volume 71, Issue 4 (1995): p. 418.

3 Jason Britton, "Sharon Creech: Everyday Journeys." *Publishers Weekly*. Volume 248, Issue 29 (2001): p. 153.

4 Creech, "Newbery Medal Acceptance," p. 418.

5 "Sharon Creech on *Love That Dog*," Twenty by Jenny.

Chapter 2

1 Sharon Creech, "Biography." Sharon Creech Web site. http://www.sharoncreech.com/meet/bio.asp.

2 Ibid.

3 "Sharon Creech Author Program In-depth Interview: Insights Beyond the Slide Shows." Teaching Books. net. http://www.teachingbooks.net/content/Creech_qu.pdf.

4 "Sharon Creech." ACHUKA Web site. http://www.achuka.co.uk/interviews/creech.php.

5 "Sharon Creech Author Bio." Kidsreads.com. http://www.kidsreads.com/guides/heartbeat2.asp.

6 Sharon Creech Biography." Scholastic Web site. http://www2.scholastic.com/browse/contributor.jsp?id=1811.

7 Andrea Sachs, "A Writer Who's 13 At Heart." *Time*, August 19, 2001. http://www.time.com/time/magazine/article/0,9171,171808,00.html.

8 Sharon Creech, *A Fine, Fine School*. New York: HarperCollins, 2001, p. 20.

9 Creech, "Biography."

10 Ibid.

11 Judith Hendershot and Jackie Peck, "An Interview with Sharon Creech, 1995 Newbery Medal Winner." *The Reading Teacher*. Volume 49, Issue 5 (1996): p. 380.

12 Creech, "Newbery Medal Acceptance," p. 419.

13 "Author Interview: Sharon Creech." HarperTeen Web site. http://www.harperteen.com/author/AuthorExtra.aspx?displayType=interview&authorID=11974.

14 Ibid.

15 Sally Holmes Holtze, ed. *Seventh Book of Junior Authors and Illustrators*. New York: H.W. Wilson, 1996, p. 67.

16 Ibid.

17 Colleen Kearney Rich, "Interview with Alum Sharon Creech, Award-Winning Author." *Mason Gazette*,

January 7, 2008. http://gazette.gmu.
edu/articles/11320.

18 Alice B. McGinty, *Sharon Creech*.
New York: Rosen Publishing, 2005,
p. 20.

19 Sharon Creech, *Absolutely Normal
Chaos*. New York: HarperCollins,
1990, p. 121.

20 "Sharon Creech Author Program
In-depth Interview."

21 McGinty, p. 22.

22 Creech, "Biography."

23 McGinty, p. 24.

24 Hollis Lowery-Moore and Sharon
Creech, "Creating People Who
Are Quirky and Kind." *Teacher
Librarian*. Volume 28, Issue 4
(2001): p. 54.

25 "Sharon Creech Author Program
In-depth Interview."

Chapter 3

1 "Sharon Creech Author Bio."
Kidsreads.com.

2 Rich, "Interview with Alum Sharon
Creech."

3 "Meet the Writers: Sharon Creech."
Barnes & Noble Web site. http://
www.barnesandnoble.com/writers/
writerdetails.asp?z=y&cid=968047.

4 Raymond Allen, "Sharon Creech:
1995 Newbery Medal Winner."
Teaching Pre K–8. Volume 26, Issue
8 (1996): p. 48.

5 Ibid.

6 Jason Britton, "Sharon Creech:
Everyday Journeys." *Publishers
Weekly*. Volume 248, Issue 29
(2001): p. 153.

7 Lyle D. Rigg, "Sharon Creech." *The
Horn Book Magazine*. Volume 71,
Issue 4 (1995): p. 429.

8 Ibid.

9 Nicolette Jones, "Children need
a place where they can spit." *Times
of London*. http://www.times
online.co.uk/tol/life_and_style/
article1149960.ece.

10 Sharon Creech, *The Wanderer*. New
York: HarperCollins, 2000, p. 275.

11 Ibid, p. 277.

12 Jones, "Children need a place where
they can spit."

13 Creech, "Newbery Medal
Acceptance," p. 420.

14 Jones, "Children need a place where
they can spit."

15 Rigg, "Sharon Creech," p. 429.

16 Jones, "Children need a place where
they can spit."

Chapter 4

1 Rigg, "Sharon Creech," p. 429.

2 Creech, "Newbery Medal
Acceptance," p. 420.

3 Sue Donckels, "Spotlight on
Sharon Creech & her latest book
The Castle Corona." WOW!
Women on Writing Web site.
http://wow-womenonwriting.
com/14-FE-SharonCreech.html.

4 Sharon Creech, "*Absolutely Normal
Chaos*: Inspiration." Sharon Creech
Web site. http://www.sharoncreech.
com/novels/03.asp.

5 Pamela Sissi Carroll, *Sharon
Creech: Teen Reads: Student
Companions to Young Adult
Literature*. Santa Barbara, Calif.:
Greenwood Publishing Group,
2007, p. 3.

6 Hendershot and Peck, "An
Interview with Sharon Creech,"
p. 380.

7 Ibid.

8 Sharon Creech, *Walk Two Moons*. New York: HarperCollins, 1994, p. 1.

9 "Sharon Creech," ACHUKA Web site.

10 Rigg, "Sharon Creech," p. 429.

11 "*Walk Two Moons*," *Kirkus Reviews*. Volume LXII, No. 12 (1994): p. 842.

Chapter 5

1 Creech, "Newbery Medal Acceptance," p. 423.

2 "Sharon Creech Author Program In-depth Interview."

3 Britton, "Sharon Creech: Everyday Journeys," p. 154.

4 Rigg, "Sharon Creech," p. 429.

5 "Sharon Creech Author Program In-depth Interview."

6 Ibid.

Chapter 6

1 Sissi Carroll, *Sharon Creech: Teen Reads*, p. 36.

2 Creech, *Absolutely Normal Chaos*, p. 131.

3 Richard Peck, "Writing in a Straight Line." *The Horn Book Magazine*. Volume 73, Issue 5 (1997): p. 529.

4 Teri S. Lesesne, Lois Buckman, and Rosemary Chance, "Books for Adolescents—*Walk Two Moons* by Sharon Creech." *Journal of Reading*. Volume 38, Issue 6 (1995): p. 504.

5 Hal Piper, "Are the Plots of Kids' Books Too Realistic?" *Chicago Tribune*, April 21, 1995, p. 19.

6 Sharon Creech, "*Pleasing the Ghost* Inspiration." Sharon Creech Web site. http://www.sharoncreech.com/novels/05.asp.

7 Elizabeth Devereaux and Diane Roback, "*Pleasing the Ghost*." *Publishers Weekly*. Volume 243, Issue 30 (1996): p. 242.

8 Mary Jo Drungil, "*Pleasing the Ghost*." *School Library Journal*. Volume 42, Issue 11 (1996): p. 104.

9 Sharon Creech, "*Chasing Redbird* Inspiration." Sharon Creech Web site. http://sharoncreech.com/novels/04.asp.

10 Susan McCaffrey, "*Chasing Redbird*." *School Library Journal*. Volume 45, Issue 7 (1999): p. 53.

11 Pamela J. Dunston, "*Chasing Redbird*." *The Reading Teacher*. Volume 52, Issue 3 (1998): p. 276.

12 Ethel Heins, "*Chasing Redbird*." *The Horn Book Magazine*. Volume 73, Issue 3 (1997): pp. 316–317.

13 Creech, "*Chasing Redbird* Inspiration."

14 Diane Roback, Jennifer M. Brown, and Cindi Di Marzo, "*Bloomability*." *Publishers Weekly*. Volume 245, Issue 29 (1998): pp. 220–221.

15 Nancy Bond, "*Bloomability*." *The Horn Book Magazine*. Volume 74, Issue 5 (1998): pp. 605–606.

16 Sharon Creech, "*The Wanderer* Inspiration." Sharon Creech Web site. http://www.sharoncreech.com/novels/07.asp.

17 Roger Sutton, "*The Wanderer*." *The Horn Book Magazine*. Volume 76, Issue 3 (2000): p. 311.

18 Angela Schult, "*The Wanderer.*" *Voices From the Middle.* Volume 9, Issue 3 (2002); p. 55.

19 Meg Wolitzer, "*Love That Dog.*" *New York Times.* October 21, 2001, p. 30.

20 Laura Tillotson, "*Love That Dog.*" *Book Links.* Volume 11, Issue 3 (2001/2002): p. 23.

21 Patricia A. Crawford, "*A Fine, Fine School.*" *Childhood Education.* Volume 78, Issue 2 (2001/2002): p. 110.

22 Jones, "Children need a place where they can spit."

23 Caroline Horn, "Carnegie Needs Trade Support." *Bookseller.* Issue 5086.

24 Traci Todd, "*Granny Torrelli Makes Soup.*" *Booklist.* Volume 100, Issue 11 (2004): p. 990.

25 Sharon Creech, "*Granny Torrelli Makes Soup* Inspiration." Sharon Creech Web site. http://sharoncreech.com/novels/12.asp.

26 Karen Coats, "*Granny Torrelli Makes Soup.*" *Bulletin of the Center for Children's Books.* Volume 57, Issue 2 (2003): p. 55.

27 Lester L. Laminack and Barbara H. Bell, "*Granny Torrelli Makes Soup.*" *Language Arts.* Volume 82, Issue 3 (2005): p. 226.

28 "Author Interview: Sharon Creech." HarperCollins Web site. http://www.harpercollins.com/author/authorExtra.aspx?authorID=11974&displayType=interview.

29 Sharon Creech, "*Replay* Inspiration." Sharon Creech Web site. http://sharoncreech.com/novels/15.asp.

30 "Author Interview: Sharon Creech." HarperCollins Web site.

31 Sharon Creech, "*The Castle Corona* Inspiration." Sharon Creech Web site. http://sharoncreech.com/novels/16.asp.

32 Jennifer Mattson, "*The Castle Corona.*" *Booklist.* Volume 104, Issue 1 (2007): p. 113.

33 Susan Dove Lempke, "*The Castle Corona.*" *The Horn Book Magazine.* Volume 83, Issue 6 (2007): p. 675.

34 Karen Coats, "*The Castle Corona.*" *Bulletin of the Center for Children's Books.* Volume 61, Issue 3 (2007): p. 135.

35 Susan Dove Lempke, "*Hate That Cat.*" *The Horn Book Magazine.* Volume 84, Issue 6 (2008): p. 699.

36 Thom Barthelmess, "*Hate That Cat.*" *Booklist.* Volume 104, Issue 22 (2008): p. 70.

37 Meghan Cox Gurdon, "*The Unfinished Angel.*" *Wall Street Journal.* http://online.wsj.com/article/SB1000142405274870329800457445996329952922 94.html.

38 "*The Unfinished Angel.*" Library Thing Web site. http://www.librarything.com/work/8201567/reviews.

Chapter 7

1 Claire Kirch, "A New Moon for Sharon Creech." *Publishers Weekly.* Volume 251, Issue 16 (2004): p. 26.

2 Julie Salamon, "A Children's Troupe, Homeward Bound." *New York Times*, July 8, 2005, p. E1.

3 Justin Chanda, "Introduction," *Acting Out: Six One-Act Plays! Six*

Newbery Stars! New York: Simon & Schuster, 2008, p. xiii.

4 Karen Coats, "*Acting Out!*" *Bulletin of the Center for Children's Books.* Volume 62, Issue 1 (2008): p. 10.

5 Kristine Wildner, "*Acting Out: Six One-Act Plays! Six Newbery Stars!*" *Library Media Connection.* Volume 27, Issue 2 (2008): p. 91.

Chapter 8

1 Neela Sakaria, "Sharon Creech, Newbery Medal winner and author of *Love That Dog.*" BookWire Web site. http://www.bookwire.com/bookwire/MeettheAuthor/Interview_Sharon_Creech.htm.

2 Donckels, "Spotlight on Sharon Creech & her latest book *The Castle Corona.*"

3 Hendershot and Peck, "An Interview with Sharon Creech, p. 381."

4 Sharon Creech, "The Colors of a Draft." Words We Say blog. http://sharonkaycreech.blogspot.com/2010/02/colors-of-draft.html.

5 Creech, "Sharon Creech: In Her Own Words."

6 Creech, "Newbery Medal Acceptance," p. 424.

7 Hendershot and Peck, "An Interview with Sharon Creech," p. 382.

8 "Sharon Creech." ACHUKA Web site.

9 Kearney Rich, "Interview with Alum Sharon Creech, Award-Winning Author."

10 Donckels, "Spotlight on Sharon Creech & her latest book *The Castle Corona.*"

11 Ibid.

12 "Author Interview: Sharon Creech." HarperTeen Web site.

13 Donckels, "Spotlight on Sharon Creech & her latest book *The Castle Corona.*"

14 Britton, "Sharon Creech: Everyday Journeys," p. 154.

15 "Teach Creech! Using Literature Circles." Sharon Creech Web site. http://sharoncreech.com/teach/teach-creech.pdf.

16 Marta S. Segal, "Stepping through *Walk Two Moons.*" *Book Links.* Volume 11, Issue 5 (2002): p. 37.

17 Barbara Feinberg, "Summer Reading List Blues." *New York Times*, July 18, 2004. http://www.nytimes.com/2004/07/18/opinion/summer-reading-list-blues.html.

18 "Sharon Creech." ACHUKA Web site.

19 Peter Thacker, "Speaking My Mind: Growing Beyond Circumstance: Have We Overemphasized Hopelessness in Young Adult Literature?" *English Journal* (High School edition). Volume 96, Issue 3 (2007): p. 17.

20 Ibid.

WORKS BY
SHARON CREECH

1990 *Absolutely Normal Chaos*
1994 *Walk Two Moons*
1996 *Pleasing the Ghost*
1997 *Chasing Redbird*
1998 *Bloomability*
2000 *The Wanderer*
2001 *Love That Dog; A Fine, Fine School*
2002 *Ruby Holler*
2003 *Granny Torrelli Makes Soup*
2004 *Heartbeat*
2005 *Replay*
2006 *Who's That Baby?*
2007 *The Castle Corona*
2008 *Hate That Cat*
2009 *The Unfinished Angel*

POPULAR BOOKS

LOVE THAT DOG

Creech's first book in verse is the story of Jack and the dog that he has lost. In poems that are encouraged by his teacher, Miss Stretchberry, Jack reveals his emotions and deals with his loss. Jack is inspired by one particular poet, Walter Dean Myers, and invites the poet to visit his class.

RUBY HOLLER

Ruby Holler is the home of Tiller and Sairy, who are looking to invite adventure into their lives. When orphaned twins Dallas and Florida come into their lives from the foster care system, the adventure becomes one that they did not quite expect, but one that all four of them find enjoyable. *Ruby Holler* won the Carnegie Medal, which is a British award for excellence in children's literature, similar to the Newbery.

WALK TWO MOONS

Thirteen-year-old Salamanca Tree Hiddle travels to Idaho with her grandparents. Along the way, she tells them the story of her friend Phoebe Winterbottom and her disappearing mother. She also reveals that Phoebe's story parallels her own as she, too, searches for her own mother. *Walk Two Moons* won the Newbery Medal.

THE WANDERER

Using journal entries and alternating the perspective between protagonist Sophie and her cousin Cody, Creech tells the story of six sailors who are crossing the Atlantic from Connecticut to Ireland. The book is about what they all discover about themselves and the sea along the way. *The Wanderer* was named a Newbery Honor book.

POPULAR CHARACTERS

DALLAS AND FLORIDA

The two are called the "trouble twins" at their foster home, where they spend a lot of time in the Thinking Corner, wearing I've Been Bad shirts, and dreaming up ways to run away. When they meet Sairy and Tiller Morey, they finally find a home with this older couple who are looking for one last adventure.

JACK

The protagonist of *Love That Dog* is dealing with the loss of a beloved pet. He is gently encouraged by his teacher to put his feelings down in poetry. Though Jack is reluctant at first, he finds that by emulating the style of great poets, he is able to deal with the loss in his life.

SALAMANCA TREE HIDDLE

"Sal" is the protagonist of *Walk Two Moons.* In the book, she embarks on a cross-country trip with her grandparents to discover the path that her mother took over a year earlier, just before she disappeared. Part Native American, Sal passes time on her trip telling stories about her friend, who also lost a mother, as she has.

SOPHIE

Sophie is the only female crew member on the ship *The Wanderer.* During the trans-Atlantic sailing trip, Sophie tells stories about her grandfather and tries to confront a tragic incident in her past, which also happened in the ocean and now comes flooding back.

MAJOR AWARDS

1995 *Absolutely Normal Chaos* is the named to the 100 Best Books Reading and Sharing, New York Public Library; Creech wins the Newbery Medal for *Walk Two Moons.*

1997 She is ranked on the ALA Best Books of 1997 for *Chasing Redbird.*

1999 Creech is placed on the IRA Young Adult Choice List for *Chasing Redbird* and the IRA/CBC Children's Choices for *Bloomability.*

2001 Creech wins the Christopher Award for *The Wanderer*; the Newbery Honor Award for *The Wanderer*; the Christopher Award for *Love That Dog*; and the Claudia Lewis Poetry Award for *Love That Dog.*

2002 She wins the Carnegie Medal for *Ruby Holler.*

2004 *Granny Torrelli Makes Soup* is named to the Notable Children's Books, ALA-ALSC.

2005 *Replay* is named to the 100 Best Books for Reading and Sharing, New York Public Library.

BIBLIOGRAPHY

Allen, Raymond. "Sharon Creech: 1995 Newbery Medal Winner." *Teaching Pre K–8* Volume 26, Issue 8 (1996): p. 48.

"Author Interview: Sharon Creech." HarperCollins Web site. Available online. URL: http://www.harpercollins.com/author/authorExtra.aspx?authorID=11974&displayType=interview.

"Author Interview: Sharon Creech." HarperTeen Web site. Available online. URL: http://www.harperteen.com/author/AuthorExtra.aspx?displayType=interview&authorID=11974.

Barthelmess, Thom. "*Hate That Cat.*" *Booklist* Volume 104, Issue 22 (2008): p. 70.

Beetz, Kirk H. and Suzanne Niemeyer, eds. *Beacham's Guide to Literature for Young Adults.* Florence, Ky.: Cengage Learning, 2001.

Bond, Nancy. "*Bloomability.*" *The Horn Book Magazine* Volume 74, Issue 5 (1998): pp. 605–606.

Bostrom, Kathleen Long. *Winning Authors: Profiles of the Newbery Medalists.* Westport, Conn.: Libraries Unlimited, 2003.

Britton, Jason. "Sharon Creech: Everyday Journeys." *Publishers Weekly* Volume 248, Issue 29 (2001): p. 153.

Carroll, Pamela Sissi. *Sharon Creech: Teen Reads: Student Companions to Young Adult Literature.* Santa Barbara, Calif.: Greenwood Publishing Group, 2007.

Coats, Karen. "*Acting Out!*" *Bulletin of the Center for Children's Books* Volume 62, Issue 1 (2008): p. 10.

———. "*Granny Torrelli Makes Soup.*" *Bulletin of the Center for Children's Books* Volume 57, Issue 2 (2003): p. 55.

———. "*The Castle Corona.*" *Bulletin of the Center for Children's Books* Volume 61, Issue 3 (2007): p. 135.

Crawford, Patricia A. "*A Fine, Fine School.*" *Childhood Education* Volume 78, Issue 2 (2001/2002): p. 110.

Creech, Sharon. *A Fine, Fine School.* New York: HarperCollins, 2001.

———. *Absolutely Normal Chaos.* New York: HarperCollins, 1990.

————. "Newbery Medal Acceptance." *The Horn Book Magazine* Volume 71, Issue 4 (1995): pp. 418–421.

————. "Sharon Creech: In Her Own Words." BookBrowse. Available online. URL: http://www.bookbrowse.com/author_interviews/full/index.cfm?author_number=448.

————. *Walk Two Moons.* New York: HarperCollins, 1994.

————. *The Wanderer.* New York: HarperCollins, 2000.

Devereaux, Elizabeth, and Diane Roback. "*Pleasing the Ghost.*" *Publishers Weekly* Volume 243, Issue 30 (1996): p. 242.

Donckels, Sue. "Spotlight on Sharon Creech & her latest book *The Castle Corona.*" WOW! Women on Writing Web site. Available online. URL: http://wow-womenonwriting.com/14-FE-SharonCreech.html.

Drungil, Mary Jo. "*Pleasing the Ghost.*" *School Library Journal* Volume 42, Issue 11 (1996): p. 104.

Dunston, Pamela J. "*Chasing Redbird.*" *The Reading Teacher* Volume 52, Issue 3 (1998): p. 276.

Feinberg, Barbara. "Summer Reading List Blues." *New York Times*, July 18, 2004. Available online. URL: http://www.nytimes.com/2004/07/18/opinion/summer-reading-list-blues.html.

Gurdon, Meghan Cox. "*The Unfinished Angel.*" *Wall Street Journal.* Available online: URL: http://online.wsj.com/article/SB10001424052748703298004574459632995292294.html.

Harrison, Barbara, and Gregory Maguire, eds. *Origins of Story: On Writing for Children.* New York: Simon & Schuster, 1999.

Heins, Ethel. "*Chasing Redbird.*" *The Horn Book Magazine* Volume 73, Issue 3 (1997): pp. 316–317.

Hendershot, Judith, and Jackie Peck. "An Interview with Sharon Creech, 1995 Newbery Medal Winner." *The Reading Teacher* Volume 49, Issue 5 (1996): p. 380.

Holtze, Sally Holmes, ed. *Seventh Book of Junior Authors and Illustrators.* New York: H.W. Wilson, 1996.

Horn, Caroline. "Carnegie Needs Trade Support." *Bookseller* Issue 5086.

Jones, Nicolette. "Children need a place where they can spit." *Times* of London. Available online. URL: http://www.timesonline.co.uk/tol/life_and_style/article1149960.ece.

Kirch, Claire. "A New Moon for Sharon Creech." *Publishers Weekly* Volume 251, Issue 16 (2004): p. 26.

Laminack, Lester L., and Barbara H. Bell. "*Granny Torrelli Makes Soup.*" *Language Arts* Volume 82, Issue 3 (2005): p. 226.

Lempke, Susan Dove. "*Hate That Cat.*" *The Horn Book Magazine* Volume 84, Issue 6 (2008): p. 699.

———. "*The Castle Corona.*" *The Horn Book Magazine* Volume 83, Issue 6 (2007): p. 675.

Lesesne, Teri S., Lois Buckman, and Rosemary Chance. "Books for Adolescents—*Walk Two Moons* by Sharon Creech." *Journal of Reading* Volume 38, Issue 6 (1995): p. 504.

Lowery-Moore, Hollis, and Sharon Creech. "Creating People Who Are Quirky and Kind." *Teacher Librarian* Volume 28, Issue 4 (2001): p. 54.

Mattson, Jennifer. "*The Castle Corona.*" *Booklist* Volume 104, Issue 1 (2007): p. 113.

McCaffrey, Susan. "*Chasing Redbird.*" *School Library Journal* Volume 45, Issue 7 (1999): p. 53.

McGinty, Alice B. *Sharon Creech*. New York: Rosen Publishing, 2005.

"Meet the Writer: Sharon Creech," Barnes & Noble Web site. Available online. URL: http://www.barnesandnoble.com/writers/writerdetails. asp?z=y&cid=968047.

Peck, Richard. "Writing in a Straight Line." *The Horn Book Magazine* Volume 73, Issue 5 (1997): pp. 529–533.

Piper, Hal. "Are the Plots of Kids' Books Too Realistic?" *Chicago Tribune*, April 21, 1995, p. 19.

Rich, Colleen Kearney. "Interview with Alum Sharon Creech, Award-Winning Author." *Mason Gazette,* January 7, 2008. Available online. URL: http://gazette.gmu.edu/articles/11320.

Rigg, Lyle D. "Sharon Creech." *The Horn Book Magazine* Volume 71, Issue 4 (1995): p. 429.

Roback, Diane, Jennifer M. Brown, and Cindi Di Marzo. "*Bloomability.*" *Publishers Weekly* Volume 245, Issue 29 (1998): pp. 220–221.

Sachs, Andrea. "A Writer Who's 13 At Heart." *Time*, August 19, 2001. Available online. URL: http://www.time.com/time/magazine/ article/0,9171,171808,00.html.

Sadaria, Neela. "Sharon Creech, Newbery Medal winner and author of Love That Dog" BookWire. Available online. URL: http://www. bookwire.com/bookwire/MeettheAuthor/Interview_Sharon_Creech. htm.

Salamon, Julie. "A Children's Troupe, Homeward Bound." *New York Times*, July 8, 2005, p. E1.

Schult, Angela. "*The Wanderer.*" *Voices From the Middle* Volume 9, Issue 3 (2002): p. 55.

Segal, Marta S. "Stepping through *Walk Two Moons.*" *Book Links* Volume 11, Issue 5 (2002): p. 37.

"Sharon Creech," ACHUKA Web site. Available online. URL: http://www.achuka.co.uk/interviews/creech.php.

"Sharon Creech Author Bio." Kidsreads.com. Available online. URL: http://www.kidsreads.com/authors/au-creech-sharon.asp.

"Sharon Creech Author Program In-depth Interview: Insights Beyond the Slide Shows." Teaching Books.net. Available online. URL: http://www.teachingbooks.net/content/Creech_qu.pdf.

"Sharon Creech on *Love That Dog.*" Twenty by Jenny. Available online. URL: http://www.youtube.com/watch?v=9atmYRlEzCM.

Sutton, Roger. "*The Wanderer.*" *The Horn Book Magazine* Volume 76, Issue 3 (2000): p. 311.

Thacker, Peter. "Speaking My Mind: Growing Beyond Circumstance: Have We Overemphasized Hopelessness in Young Adult Literature?" *English Journal* (High School edition) Volume 96, Issue 3 (2007): p. 17.

"*The Unfinished Angel.*" Library Thing Web site. Available online. URL: http://www.librarything.com/work/8201567/reviews.

Tillotson, Laura. "*Love That Dog.*" *Book Links* Volume 11, Issue 3 (2002): p. 23.

Todd, Traci. "*Granny Torrelli Makes Soup.*" *Booklist* Volume 100, Issue 11 (2004): p. 990.

"*Walk Two Moons.*" *Kirkus Reviews* Volume LXII, No. 12 (1994): p. 842.

Wildner, Kristine. "*Acting Out: Six One-Act Plays! Six Newbery Stars!*" *Library Media Connection* Volume 27, Issue 2 (2008): p. 91.

Wolitzer, Meg. "*Love That Dog.*" *New York Times*, October 21, 2001, p. 30.

FURTHER READING

Books

Drew, Bernard A. *100 More Popular Young Adult Authors: Biographical Sketches and Bibliographies.* Greenwood Village, Colo.: Libraries Unlimited, 2002.

Tighe, Mary Ann. *Sharon Creech: The Words We Choose to Say.* Lanham, Md.: Scarecrow Press, Inc., 2006.

Web Sites

Sharon Creech's Official Website
http://www.sharoncreech.com

Sharon Creech Website—UK
http://www.sharoncreech.co.uk/

Words We Say: Sharon Creech's Blog
http://sharonkaycreech.blogspot.com

PICTURE CREDITS

INDEX

Note: characters are listed by first name, with the title of the work in which they appear in parentheses.

ABOUT THE CONTRIBUTOR

TRACEY BAPTISTE enjoys writing books for young adults. She is the author of six books, including a biography of Stephenie Meyer. In 2005, her debut novel, *Angel's Grace*, was named one of the 100 best books for reading and sharing, along with Sharon Creech's *Replay*. Her favorite Creech book is *Love That Dog*. You can find out more about Ms. Baptiste on her Web site, www.traceybaptiste.com.